DOT DOT DOT

by Renata Semba

The contents of this book are a recommendation only and the author takes no responsibility regarding the use and application of any of the suggested treatments. Acordingly, this book should not be substituted for the advise of your doctor or any other licenced health care professional. Before starting on any diet it is recommended to see your medical practioner.

Designed by Kristin Stelling, www.fundus-design.com

BIOGRAPHY

Renata Semba is one of Europe's leading makeup artists who works in the fashion, film and advertising industries. She originally studied anatomy, physiology and nutrition, going on to work in a naturopathic clinic which has given her a unique insight into the typical health and well being issues faced by models.

Inspired by her parents who were both hairdressers, Renata went on to study design and makeup extensively, specializing in makeup for film and television. Put all this together with over 20 years as a professional hair and makeup artist and you have an individual who can speak with authority on the specific needs of models.

Travelling all over the world on photo shoots and working with the world's foremost models, stylists and photographers has given her an insight into all the tricks and tips of the trade which she now shares with her colleagues in this book.

Her straightforward approach appeals to those who are looking for effective, simple solutions to some of the beauty and business problems faced by models.

Dot Dot Dot is destined to be an industry bible and a must have for those wanting to start their business life on the right foot!

DEDICATION

To my Mum who inspired me to be all the person I could be. In the face of predjudice, adversity and impossible odds, she rose to the occassion with dignity and intelligence. I would be proud to be half the woman you are, thank you for being such amazing role model and giving me so much love, support and encouragement.

To my girlfriends, not all models but all stunningly beautiful in my eyes. I love you all, but must mention Dawn and Natalie. Your love, beauty, intelligence and power as women make me feel honored to count myself as your friend. Your continuous giving and reaching down to lift up and inspire those around you, makes you great and I want to let you know that I think you are remarkable women.

To all the wonderful, funny, smart, loving and brave models I haven't met yet and all those I will never get to meet. This book offers you the information to give you an edge over the others in this competitive business but most importantly, I hope it helps you to take yourself and your job seriously enough to make a great start in your life. Be aware your memories are todays experiences, make them great!

„It is more important to look fresh than perfect"

„It's not what happens to you it's how you deal with it"

„Women should look like they smell good"

„Be all the person you can be"

„It is more important to be the right person than to find the right person"

„A great base makes a great face"

„Do your best, perfection is transient"

„Live below your means, above the average and up to your standards"

TABLE OF CONTENTS

INTRODUCTION

As a professional model you truly are a citizen of the world and an ambassador of your home country.

RESPONSIBILITIES AS A MODEL

Everyone that you come in contact with will hold you up as an example of Russians, Americans or whatever, but also as an example of all that others in the world aspire to be. You are young, beautiful and live a privileged life. I know some of you reading this will be wondering when the privileges are going to start, but in all seriousness, you have probably had very little or limited experience in any other job, other than modelling, and are still hopefully naive to the hardships and trials life's lessons can bring. Hopefully you can gain a head start from Dot Dot Dot, so it is suggested to enjoy your freedom, success, youth and beauty while you have it, but use it wisely because it will not all last forever. By treating modelling as a business you will be able to enjoy it and have as much success as possible and gain many lifelong advantages out of the experience. You will meet a lot of amazing people, and learn of the sweetness and bitterness life can bring, because you will be living a very intense life.

This book is designed to give you some unbiased, helpful signposts for your journey. Many people will offer you their advice along the way in addition to this book and it would be wise to listen, consider the information and learn.

In return for this fabulous life, there is quite a lot expected of you. As in life in general, it is not absolutely necessary to do certain things.

Some things will be fine as they are, some areas you will need to work on to improve, and some things will be difficult for you to change but rewarding in the end.

Your grooming as a model is of utmost importance, along with your figure and easy-to-get-along-with personality. You have to be prepared to work hard, work together with a team and concentrate on your job. Your bad temper, stubbornness or bitchiness will only show others you are immature and unable to cope with the amount of responsibility you have been given. Absolutely no one is interested in immature, negative, lazy or unco-operative models, or for that fact, people. If you recognize any of these traits within yourself, start now to discipline yourself. When you recognize negative behaviour, try to throw a switch in your head, which makes you behave in the opposite way, but which achieves the exact same outcome. (See Chapter on Bad Habits)

As in all things, doing your very best with all the information you have is all that anyone will expect of you. All the information you will need as a model is contained in this book. All other information you gather along the way from your experiences is extra, and it will give you a rich source of knowledge to use on your life journey. Good luck!

GROOM

Establishing your grooming habits may seem like a hassle at first as you imagine they will take up so much of your free time.

Start off by including the standard things you should be doing as a matter of course, such as using a deodorant that doesn't leave a white residue either under your arm (not attractive in photographs!!) or on expensive designer clothes. Other things will be noticed in the long run and will be up to you to form as a habit. In other words, don't even imagine that you have a choice in the matter when it comes to taking off your makeup.

If you are coming home after a late night out, take off your coat, change your clothes, wash your face, brush your teeth and any other necessities before you do anything else. If you sit in front of the TV you may fall asleep.

In fact, by doing ANYTHING before washing your face, you create a moment for thinking "Ugh! Now I have to get up and go and wash my face" Don't even get into the habit of CREATING the moments for such thoughts, then you will never resent the fact that you have to wash your face before sleep or bed. If you are coming home from the studio and haven't already completely removed your makeup for the train ride home, (remember: absolutely, completely remove your makeup before bed or sleep) do it immediately upon coming home so NOTHING comes between you and your professional habits. By establishing these rules from the beginning, you will avoid being tempted into not doing them.

To make getting into good habits easier, choose a convenient time and place to do things when you think of it. Keep your dot dot dot lip salve / hand lotion in a drawer where you can easily use it when watching TV. This is a perfect time to allow things to soak in for ages before touching something. Another example is to do your nails in front of the TV on a Sunday night. You can hear what is going on, and it is just a matter of looking up when something exciting is happening in the movie.

The few minutes you have to wait between steps flies by and at the end, your nails are looking fabulous! Remember to use a good light, otherwise you may wake up the next day and they are NOT as fabulous as you thought last night.

Turn up the grooming, but turn DOWN the styling.

ING

Leave plenty of time for the varnish to dry before hitting the sheets as you may wake up with sheet prints in your nails. Watching TV is also a good time for a face-mask; just make sure you keep an eye on the time!!

Keep Aloe Vera gel in the bathroom so it is right at hand for any small cuts or to smooth over freshly shaved legs before you use your moisturizer. Make things convenient so you are more likely to do them. Creating routines that are convenient will assure your success in forming good habits and breaking old, bad habits that tax your energy.

It sounds simple, but integrating all the small points you learn from this book will make a huge difference in your presentation. It is not enough to know the information. You have to USE THE INFORMATION for it to be effective!!

How you organise your time for your grooming habits is obviously up to you, but being well groomed is a factor that may never be commented on directly to your face, but it is without question something that others notice, admire and will respect you for. Not only is it a sign to others that you are disciplined and have self-respect, but it will also say that you are serious about your profession and the way you present yourself.

The state of your skin, hair and nails plays an integral part in the decision of your clients to make a booking and can give you the edge with your clients, bookers, hair and makeup stylists and photographers.

Do not confuse grooming with styling. Grooming is being clean and taken care of, like you would polish a glass. Styling is how you dress / accessorise and do your makeup and hair.

Everyone likes to make a good impression but the best advice anyone can give you is; turn up the grooming, but turn DOWN the styling, especially as a fashion model. "Cool", is a very important part of modelling. Making a good impression upon strangers, whether they are clients, agents or other models at castings, is part of the process.

Do not dress to over impress. It is best to be casual with your style and not look like you tried too hard or are paying too much attention to the fashion magazines. Remember to dress comfortably, especially if you are doing castings and go sees.

Don't wear heels that are too high otherwise your client will assume you only had one appointment or you love pain, both are not good! Grooming should be at full volume, beautiful skin, clean shiny hair and immaculate nails.

Before jobs and on trips is the time to catch up on any grooming necessities. Trips are perfect, as you have free evening time in the hotel for long baths, face/hair masks and manicure / pedicures.

Just remember -
NO EXPERIMENTS PLEASE!!!

SKIN

Taking good care of your skin can be one of **the most important responsibilities** of a model, besides your figure and health.

Of course the state of your health will be directly mirrored by your skin so eating a healthy, well balanced diet including fresh fruit and vegetables and plenty of still water, will make taking care of your skin much easier, and for a model should be priority number one. (See diet)

As a model you will certainly have youth on your side and your ability to use this to your maximum benefit will be the edge you will have in a very competitive market. Adding that extra glow to your skin will be that special something that will remain in the minds of your clients when they make their booking decisions.

When talking about skin, it is important not to just think about the face and pimples as your major concern. The skin is the body's largest organ, just as the liver and kidneys are organs of the body. You don't have to understand the complete physiology of the body, to take good care of it, but there are some important points to understand so you don't forget what the body needs to function well. When those points are taken care of, your maintenance becomes much easier.

The skin is not just a neat package that keeps your insides in, as mentioned above, it is the body's largest organ. It is an eliminative organ, helps regulate temperature and has an efficient process of feeding itself with oils and substances that protect and soften the skin.

Your job is not to disrupt this process too drastically and supplement it when your circumstances warrant.

SKIN BRUSHING

Skin brushing should be done every morning before you shower, on dry skin. Skin brushes should NOT be shared and should be made from natural fibres. They are inexpensive and can be found in a variety of shapes and forms such as mittens and long handled brushes in stores such as The Body Shop, pharmacies and drug stores. Do not use body brushes in the shower or gloves made of synthetic fibres. Do not use body brushes for, or on the face, they are for the body only. Replace your body brush regularly, about every 6-8 months.

Brush the skin gently at first, until your skin becomes more accustomed to the brush. Long sweeping movements towards the heart will stimulate blood flow, bringing the nutrients and oxygen in the blood to all areas of the skin. Dead skin cells will be sloughed off as well as soap residues so the skin will be better able to "breathe".

Another important part of skin brushing, and the reason for the sweeping movements towards the heart, is the stimulation of the lymphatic flow. Lymphatic fluid is the waste product produced by the cells, which should be carried out of the tissues by the lymphatic system and filtered underneath the collarbones.

The lymphatic system relies on peristaltic movement (spontaneous muscle contraction) and muscle contraction from exercise. By encouraging the flow of lymphatic fluids you keep the tissues free of the waste products that can cause puffiness in the body as well as cellulite. Start your brush strokes from the feet and legs moving up the body. Finish your shower by running the water cold until it quickens your breath. This will stimulate not only the skin but also the muscles, giving your skin good tone. Don't put your face under the cold water if you are prone to broken capillaries.

SKIN CLEANSING

Using a mild soap or body gel is usually the best body cleanser but if your skin is prone to drying out and becoming itchy, use something even milder such as Eucerine Dry Skin Relief Shower & Bath Therapy (Duschlotion in Germany) and reducing the temperature of the water.In London try E45 range or anything with a neutral PH. Hot water can irritate the skin and cause it to become itchy. You should always keep hot water off the face as it can cause broken capillaries that are seen as red veins or small red spots on the face. If you have a family history of broken capillaries, keep away from saunas, extremes of temperatures (hot AND cold) and high- pressure water on the face.

It is extremely important to clean every last bit of makeup off the face and eyelashes before going to bed. Use a Q-tip dipped in eye makeup remover to get at the roots of the lashes, top and bottom.

Sleep time is when the body rejuvenates and repairs the damage from the day, so makeup residue can inhibit the natural repair and rejuvenating process of the skin, putting you behind for the next day. Puffy eyes, and pimples is what you are asking for if this rule is broken.

It is also best to try to sleep with fresh air circulating in the room, even if it means adding an extra blanket or pyjamas, as the skin will benefit from the fresh oxygen in the air. If your skin is oily it is "ok" not to use a moisturizer before bed but use a light one with a hydrating action during the day as all skins can benefit from extra hydration, sun protection factor and a film between your skin and the daily pollution.

Your choice of cleanser is important, as you need one that will do the job without too much fuss and rubbing. Try Jade Mabelline waterproof eye makeup remover. It is especially kind to sensitive eyes and quickly dissolves even heavy eye makeup. Remember, every time you pull and rub at your skin, especially your eye area, you are adding to the stretching of the skin. Over time, this adds up to more wrinkles, so establishing a routine that is easy, gentle and automatic will serve you well over the years. Getting into gentle, but thorough skin cleansing habits will have conserved the valuable elasticity of the skin. Even patting your face dry after a shower, instead of vigorously rubbing it up and down, can add up to thousands of saved stretches of the skin. So take care of your skin as it is one of your greatest assets, be gentle! Treating your skin as the precious, beautiful thing that it is will remind you everyday to be thankful and respectful of your beauty.

MOISTURIZING

The cosmetics industry have supplied an unending amount of moisturizers for you to choose from but the most expensive of which, is not always necessarily the best, so bear that in mind when shopping for moisturizer.

Your skin should always feel a little moist to the touch. If it is dry to the touch you may need a moisturizer that has a richer texture or a higher "fat" value so the skin will stay moistened, helping to keep it soft and to discourage fine lines. Some fat in a face cream is fine especially in the winter months, if your skin is normal. If you are in your teens, you may consider your skin to be oily but this may change in the winter or as your hormones stabilize.

Specialized night cremes can enhance the body`s rejuvinating process. Try Guerlain Midnight Secret late night recovery treatment for a visible improvement.

When buying any kind of cosmetic, ask the sales assistant for samples. They are convenient for trips or when you have run out of your regular moisturizer or, if you just want to try something new. Look at the ingredients and remember that such ingredients as paraffin are responsible for making your skin feel silky and smooth and names such as petroleum are synthetic, which tend to create a chemical film on the skin and will not allow your skin to "breathe". AHAS are alpha hydroxy acids and denote a variety of naturally occurring components of sugar cane (glycolic acid) apples, (malic acid) and milk (lactic acid). These ingredients work on a molecular level to encourage the skin to turn over or regenerate faster.

This can be a great benefit to improving the texture and evenness of the skin.

It is best to take your supply of face moisturizer for the day out of the jar with a spatula and put it on your hand before applying it to the face as the finger can transfer bacteria into the jar with every application, causing the moisturizer to lose it's potency over the months it takes to finish it. Some brands cleverly have containers that dose the moisturizer out in a pump action bottle. A face moisturizer should be applied minimally to the face and soak immediately in without much rubbing. Try to imagine the fine layer of oil your face would naturally have, and give your face the minimum requirement of moisturizer, imitating the skins own oils. In this case, less is more, you are just giving it enough to trap in the body's own moisture and protect the skin from the environment. An invigorating and tingling tapping motion is also a good application technique, as it stimulates the underlying muscle without rubbing the skin. Don't hit too hard, especially if you are prone to broken capillaries (small red spots, often close to the skin around the eyes and on the cheeks.) An eye creme or gel should be placed on the pads of your two ring fingers and patted around the orbits of the eyes (the circle around the eye where the eye skin joins the face skin and just above the eyebrow)

Don't be tempted to use your eye product on the eye skin itself,

as this skin has a different structure to the rest of the face and is tissue paper fine. This skin doesn't have any pores of it's own, it has the ability to draw in moisture from the surrounding skin. By putting your product directly onto this skin, any excess will pull at this fine skin and weigh it down, causing further bags and puffiness that, actually, is defeating the purpose of the exercise. Eye cremes can have specific calming or softening qualities so choose an eye creme that tackles your specific problem. If you don't have any specific eye area problems, you may not need one at all. Puffiness can be helped by using a cold compress or splashing cold water on them. Don't use an eye creme after a late night drinking and smokings, hoping for it to miraculously get rid of the bags, dark circles or puffiness. It doesn't work like that!

Moisturizers for the body should have a reasonable fat value as the body has fewer oil glands to supply the necessary oil to the body. It should be quickly absorbed and leave the skin feeling soft but not greasy.

When applying your moisturizer pay attention to the hands and cuticles, elbows, knees, toes and heels, not only because they need special moisture attention but also by using this time to check for any dry places that need your pumice stone attention. (See troubleshooting)

Keep a concentrated moisturizer (anything with cocoa butter) and lip treatment in a drawer close by when you are watching TV or by the bed, so you can treat your hands/feet and lips to extra attention while there is time for the product to really soak in and soften.

FACE MASKS

With a variety of face-masks on the market there is an amazing amount of variation to help every skin type. Face-masks are the most important supplement to your beauty routine and can keep your skin in check without regular visits to the beautician, as much as they are enjoyable. The trick is to recognize the signs your skin is giving you, that it needs some extra help. Listed here are some basic beauty masks and the signs to show you it is time for some help.

EXFOLIANT Exfoliation is one of the most basic skin care duties and is necessary to do at least 2-3 times a week. (Some products may be used daily, such as Dermalogicas Daily Microfoliant) It can help to stimulate blood flow, slough the skin of debris and dead skin cells, which turn over much faster on the skin of the face. It can reduce the visibility of fine lines on the face and generally improve the light reflectability of the face which means the skin becomes more glowing, not more shiny. It can stimulate the oil flow of the skin due to the exfoliation process helping to unblock clogged pores. The result of stimulating blood flow and unblocking the pores can be that the skin may feel slightly more oily, which is obviously a good thing as the skins natural oils bring with them lipids and hormones that feed and regulate the skin's function. Oils are good, until they mix with dirt and pollution. Their organic components mix with the oxygen and oxygenate, or go rancid, so it is important to wash your face before bed even if you have not had on any makeup. The skin needs to be cleaned of the dirt that has been caught in the oils before it turns bad, solidifies and blocks the pores, causing blackheads, infection and pimples. The oil that is flowing is a good thing, pores that are blocked are not.

The signs to look for if you need to bump up your exfoliating routine are; dull, grey skin, blocked pores, small lumps or bumps on the nose or a rough feeling on the skin of the nose, around the nose and cheeks.

NEVER exfoliate within the orbits of the eyes and it is also advisable to avoid the lips, as they can be too sensitive for such things.

Exfoliants come in many variations and it is up to you to choose one you like. Most of the cheaper ones are physical granulates which means they are some kind of creme that contains granules, that physically rub off the dead skin cells and stimulate the blood flow from the grainy nature of the creme.

Some important points to remember when buying an exfoliator are, particles that are "natural" like almond kernels and such, can be irregular in shape and therefore can scratch, poke and irritate a sensitive skin or even aggravate your skin long before you are finished with the product. It is best to invest in one that has a combination action with salicylic acid and regular particles that will roll and lift the dead skin cells gently off. If your skin is dry, thin and sensitive, try Clarins Doux Peeling twice a week.

HYDRATING   Masks that offer an intense hydrating action are ones specifically designed for dry skins but can be just as valuable to oily skins because oily skinned people tend to strip away at the oil, forgetting that the oil is a natural inhibitor to moisture loss.

The best way to hydrate your skin is naturally, from the inside out with water, but protecting the skin from moisture loss is also of benefit to the skin.

To hydrate the skin, is to add moisture so you can expect a hydrator to make the face look fresh, pores refined or smaller and the skin slightly plumped.

Signs you need a hydrating treatment; dry, fine lines on the skin, open pores and rough and dry to the touch. Remember, the skin should always feel slightly moist.

Weleda have a face-mask with almond oil for sensitive skins that you can try. Also good for dry skins is Masque Creme from Channel. It is an intense moisturizing mask, which, when used directly after an exfolient mask will reap the maximum moisturizing benefits.

MINERAL   An essential mask, especially for oilier skins and pimple prone skin, is a mineral mask, as it absorbs impurities and allows the skin to absorb its minerals, which help to disinfect and heal spots. Some finer skins may be sensitive to the sometimes astringic action of these masks so check the ingredients for alcohol or do a patch test on the inside of your elbow to check for possible reactions.

Some mineral masks dry a little like a clay mask would, this will help to draw out impurities.

Keep your fingers away from spots and pimples and they should be gone the next day. It is best to use a mineral mask once or twice a week or when the skin is looking tired and a bit lack lustre. NEVER use a mineral mask on broken skin or in the eye area.

Try Clarins Masque Purifiant. You may even like to spot treat pimples with this mask.

CLAY   Similar to the mineral mask but more drying and not as nutrient rich, these masks are designed for thick oily skins, with a tendency to break out. Clay masks can be used only on the spots if you only have one or two, without drying out the rest of the face. The clay draws out and absorbs impurities, while drying out the spot or the oily skin. Use twice weekly if you have very oily skin but can be used purely for emergency purposes in the T zone, or once a month when the skin becomes excessively oily and you can be prone to breakouts. Try Mac's 2 in one Scrub Mask

PEEL OFF   Essentially a peel off mask is an exfoliating mask as it removes the top layer of dead skin. It can indeed be fun to peel off the mask but sensitive skins may find the pulling out of fine facial hair around the sides of the face, painful. Very often peel off masks also have a cooling or astringent quality which makes them better for thicker, oilier skins but generally speaking their fun value is the greater portion of what they have to offer. Also available are strips that you wet and apply only to the nose. When you peel them off they pull out the blackheads. Good if you are willing to wait for your nose to be covered with blackheads! Best to keep the oil flowing.

FACIALS

Having a professional facial can be a relaxing and de-stressing experience. There are all kinds of steamers and complicated looking machines at the fingertips of the Beautician but as there is not a lot of licensing or national standards it has the potential to be a brave new experience. Ask for recommendations from people who have actually been to the Beautician in question and ask for the actual name of the facialist who performed the facial treatment. Don't be afraid to ask questions before you make the appointment as the salon world has it's own language and lists of services and prices which can be quite confusing.

If the person you are talking to becomes impatient or condescending ask to speak to the facialist herself at a convenient time for you both.

It is important to be confident and informed about your beauty treatments and specialist, as this could be the person you turn to in a skin care crisis before an important job. Even trusting her/him with hot wax on your upper lip needs quite a high degree of confidence.

Ask about qualifications and any certificates that can be shown to you. Ask how long she has been working as a Beautician. (A few weeks or months is not enough) If she also does manicures and pedicures. (A good beautician will be too busy for these kinds of appointments)

Ask what products she uses and why. It is most likely she will try to encourage you to buy some products to use at home, prepare yourself for this, as it is normal and should be quite a soft sell on her part. You may mention you already have products at home that you would prefer to use up first and if she gears up into hard sell, be firm but polite, even if you simply say "NO, thank you".

When you find someone you like, be loyal and tip if it is the custom in the country you are in. Small gifts or notes of thank you are also appropriate if you are a regular. This will establish the feeling that you appreciate and value the extra care she gives to you on your visits. Should you need an appointment at short notice or have to cancel one because of a last minute booking, she will be more forgiving and understanding, as she knows you as a polite person.

Unless you need regular waxing you should visit a professional Beautician at a minimum, twice a year for a deep cleansing facial, and or any other special treatment she may offer, that you are unable to do at home. Extractions (squeezing blackheads or pimples) should be done by a professional, after a long steam, but if you insist upon doing them on yourself, the time for best results is after a long shower or bath as the skin is warm and moist and the pores open.

Always wrap tissues around your fingers and never jab the nails into the skin. If it doesn't pop easily- LEAVE IT ALONE. You will create a bigger problem than you already have by pushing it further. Violently squeezing pimples has been well documented as causing the infection to spread and go deeper into the skin, which means it is no longer a superficial infection. Being now deeper, it will be less likely to EVER "pop" and therefore will take up to three times as long to heal and more likely than not, cause deep tissue scarring. That means there will be a mark there forever. DON'T SQUEEZE PIMPLES. A Beautician will never insist with pimples but will persevere with stubborn blackheads. You may ask if she would check your back for any blemishes should you suspect any could be in an area hard to see.

DERMATOLOGISTS

When should you visit a dermatologist?
Generally speaking Dermatologists handle all skin problems that are serious. As a model, things can quickly become serious if you are losing bookings because of a problem so don't waste your time trying this and that preparation unless you definitely KNOW what the problem is, and how to solve it. In some European countries a Dermatologist is the only place you can get a glycolic peel due to the regulations and dangers of putting them in the hands of someone unqualified and not regulated.

These peels can greatly reduce early wrinkles open pores and pigmentation marks, but you will have to consider staying out of the sun in the future as the skin will be extra sensitive to the damaging rays. Some of the most common reasons to visit a Dermatologist are:

ACNE   You would not define acne as a monthly break out, but rather a constant presence of blemishes that does not seem to be affected by including fruits and vegetables in the diet and drinking plenty of water.

If you have acne, mention any medications or oral contraceptives to the dermatologist as these could likely be making you more acne prone or may affect the treatment decision of the Dermatologist. It is important that the exact name and dosage of the medication is known, so bring the medication with you if necessary.

ALLERGIC REACTIONS   If you experience a sudden redness, itching, hives or blotches, immediately discontinue any new skin care products or makeup that you feel could be responsible. If you find that it WAS the suspicious product causing the reaction, return it to the place of purchase whether you have the receipt or not (always keep cosmetic receipts for your taxation). It is most cosmetic companies' policy to return and refund products that cause allergic reactions to their customers, no questions asked. If the sales consultant is sceptical or stubborn, ask to see the manager or her supervisor and politely explain the reaction you had to the product. Supervisors are aware of company policies and consultants tend to feel defensive of their product.

If your reaction persists, discontinue all but the most simple and gentle cleansing products and make an appointment at the Dermatologist.

If you suspect it was something that a makeup artist had used on a job, try to contact their agency and leave a message and your number for them to return your call. DO NOT discuss your allergic reaction with their agency. It is normal for models to be friendly to the makeup artist and they should return your call. Explain the problem and ask the makeup artist if any other girls have had problems with the product that you suspect. This will let the makeup artist

know that this product should be viewed with suspicion, not used or that brushes should be disinfected. This is a very critical subject so be diplomatic and polite. If the makeup artist has a negative reaction you can explain the situation to your booker, and ask for a few days off to see the doctor. Your booker will then decide if the makeup artists' agent should be told.

REMOVAL OF MOLES, SKIN TAGS OR CANCERS

A Dermatologist is definitely capable of invisibly removing moles, skin tags or suspected malignancies, depending on how big or deep they are. The minute you find something new on your skin, or if you notice a mole or freckle has changed in appearance or is itchy or irritating you, make an appointment at the Dermatologist. Skin cancers can affect everyone and can progress at an alarming rate, making their way into neighbouring lymphatic nodes faster than you would imagine so do NOT procrastinate. The doctor can tell you what to look out for, what spot you have and if it should be removed for safety. Always let your doctor know you are a professional model, and make him aware you are expecting the scar to be invisible or kept absolutely minimal.

SUN CARE

Practically all moisturizers contain some kind of SPF (sun protection factor) but if you are travelling into warmer climates for work, do not expect others to bring sun protection for you to use. Apply sun protection for your face as soon as you can before going to makeup, so it has time to soak in, or bring it with you and ask the makeup artist if it is ok to apply your sunscreen before doing the makeup. Some makeup is not compatible with some sunscreens and the makeup artist may have one that she/he prefers. Normally, anything that has a gel formula and is not greasy, with the highest SPF factor you can find will be the best. Photographers do not normally shoot in the midday sun as the height of the sun creates hard shadows on the face that are unattractive, but with the use of reflectors and working outside, you may easily get more sun than you were expecting.

Be especially careful if you have a few days booked or are shooting swimsuits or summer clothes. Normally these are shot in the winter months, but a warm location can be ruthless with winter skin and accumulative sun can also result in sunburn, so better be safe than sent home! Sunburn is especially vicious on your face as it is next to impossible to cover and any kind of overexposure or sunburn will result in damage to the skin, which you should be doing your utmost to avoid.

Applying sunscreen should be done at least a half an hour before going into the sun, to give the ingredients time to activate, and should be reapplied regularly according to the instructions. Pay special attention to the sides and the back of your neck, chest, ears and top of your shoulders. Don't neglect the back of the knees, legs AND FEET. Burnt feet can be extremely painful and put you out of work just as easily as a burnt face so stay vigilant! And just so we are clear, the SPF factor should be at least30 + or a total block.

TROUBLESHOOTING

PIMPLES Woken up with a whopping pimple in the middle of your forehead the day of your big beauty shoot for Vogue? Madly squeezing it will only make it worse as it will leave a scab that will be much harder for the makeup artist to cover. Photoshop is almost always used for beauty pictures these days and if it is anything else other than beauty, the makeup artist should be able to cover it with makeup so no one would ever notice. We all know picking pimples is hard to resist, and we have all regretted doing it.

If you have the advantage of a day or so, after your shower, wrap some tissues around your two ring fingers and gently squeeze from west/east and then north /south. If it does not easily come away, take a vitamin e oil capsule, prick a hole in the end of the oil capsule with a pin or a needle and mix it with a match head size amount of crushed garlic and let it sit on the pimple for an hour or two. If it feels like it is burning your skin, you have too much garlic. When you go to bed put more Vit E oil on it and in the morning it should be on its way to disappear. Trust me, it works!

ROUGH SKIN If your heels, knees, elbows or fingers have rough, dry skin use a pumice stone to rub it away. Soak in a bath first, or put the plug in while you shower, to soak the feet, making the skin soft. Then use the pumice stone to rub off the dead skin. Vigorous movements can be used for the thick skin on the heels, but be careful with elbows as you can very quickly rub them raw! If you are careful you can also use a pumice stone for the hard dry skin around the nails on the hands and feet. If nothing helps your rough feet, include more Omega 3 oil in your diet.

If the skin on your body is rough, start by using the skin brush on dry skin (see skin brushing) then use a mild skin cleanser like Eucerine body wash and finish by NOT towel drying the skin, but rubbing liberal amounts of Weleda Calendula Skin Oil all over the body with extra attention given to knees, elbows, heels and cuticles (not recommended for the face) It has a deliciously citrus note and is the ultimate bed time accessory to soft cozy pyjamas and clean cool fresh sheets. Give it a few minutes to soak in before going to bed.

BODY PIMPLES If you find instead of one pimple on the body (which can be treated as above) a rash of small ones on the top of your arms, on your thighs or the side of calves these can be "winter skin". Basically your skin needs a good skin brushing to stimulate the blood and a bit of fresh air, sunshine and Vit B Complex. If it persists, include supplements EFA 500mcg, B Complex 50mg and Beta Carotene 15mg daily. Include more olive oil, oily fish, nuts and seeds and sprouted seeds in your diet.

FAKE TAN STRIPES   Get out your body brush or if it is really drastic try some tea tree oil or nail polish remover on a Q-tip. Only rub the very edge of the stripe to even the colour. Make a special note to not ever do it again!!

SKIN FUNGUS   If you have recently spent time on the beach and you have noticed pale circles appearing in your tan, you could have picked up a skin fungus. (See emergency health) It starts as pale circular splotches on the skin and may begin as spots on your back or arms but can quickly move to the face so don't let it develop for too long.

Generally, it is not irritating at all but could put you very quickly out of work. Use Selsun blue medicated dandruff shampoo on dry skin. Start with your arms and back in-case it stings. Rub it on and leave for 4-5 minutes to dry, and then shower off. Two or 3 days of this treatment should be enough to get rid of it but avoid your eyes and if you have it on your face just do the most general of areas i.e. cheeks forehead and neck. Avoid the eye area completely.

TOE AND FOOT FUNGUS   There are a lot of different types of fungal infections and they can have different names depending where, on the body they appear and what type of infections they are. Fungal infections can affect the body, head or groin area. Tinea pedis most often affects the feet and toes. Often called athletes foot it is practically unavoidable due to the sharing of shoes but it is easily treated with preparations from the chemist or prevented by regularly wiping the feet and toes with a Q-tip dipped in Tea Tree Oil. As an anti fungal, tea tree oil can disinfect and kill the bacteria that cause these fungal infections. DON'T use the same end of the Q-tip for both feet and DON'T dip the

Q-tip back in the Tea Tree Oil bottle once you have swabbed your toes and feet.

If you find you have the tell tale signs of itching and redness or raw skin between the toes, buy one of the easy to use preparations from the chemist. You may only need to apply some of them once but others may need to be applied once a day for a few days. Don't let this condition prevail as it is highly contagious and you will be potentially infecting others around you. (Think roommates as well as other models)

Toe nails may also be affected, so look for white patches on the nail that come off with a nail file but return a day or so later. Nails need a special treatment from the chemist and may take longer to cure. If you don't attend to them, the fungus may cause long term nail bed damage, deforming the shape of the nail.

ECZEMA   There are several different types of eczemas, some are hereditary (passed on in families) and it often runs in families who also suffer from asthma and hay fever. Eczema is sometimes called the itch that rashes. In other words, it may start off as dry skin that itches and then turns into a red scaly rash once it is scratched. Beginning as dry scaly skin in the inside of elbows, behind the knees, on the face, neck or hands, it can be brought on, or made worse by, poor diet, stress, enviromental allergens, drugs or lifestyle habits. The best treatment is to counter the things that set it off. Follow a good diet, including foods with zinc (oysters are the richest source) sunflower seeds, beans and nuts. Avoid foods that are common allergens and which can inhibit the absorbtion of zinc into the body, such as wheat and dairy. Avoid drying the skin out, so eat plenty of Omega 3 rich food (oily fish like wild salmon, sardines as well as flax seeds, sunflower seeds, walnuts and almonds) Use non drying wash lotions such as Eucerine or others that protect the skins' Ph balance. Moisurize the skin daily directly after showering to campture the moisture.

HAIR

As a professional model it is your responsibility to maintain healthy looking hair.

Combine the right maintenance regime with the appropriate products. Follow professional advise when it comes to cutting and colouring. This should make keeping your hair in perfect condition quick and easy. Treat your hair gently, without tearing or tugging at it.

SHAMPOO

Detergent based and alkaline shampoos work by swelling the hair shaft and lifting the cuticles on the hair shaft. They carry an electric charge that causes the hair strands to react with each other, producing static. After shampooing, the hair is left with a negative charge making the hair rough; conditioners contain positively charged agents that bond with the negative charge of the hair making the cuticles lie flat, and the hair more manageable and less prone to static.

If your hair feels rough and coarse after shampooing, your shampoo has a lot of detergent in it. If you wash your hair often, you might like to try one that is not so harsh. There are many different brands on the market but if you are confused, try one called an everyday shampoo, or one that says mild. Ask your favourite hair stylist which brand they recommend or just try a few until you find one you feel does not strip and dry out your hair. It should feel soft, easy to manage and not overly tangled. This means the hair will look shiny and glossy.

CONDITIONER

Designed to work within a minute or two, conditioners make the cuticles of the hair shaft lie flat, making the hair not only more manageable but more light reflective. This means the hair looks shiny and glossy. Conditioners should always be used after shampooing to make your hair soft, manageable and shiny.

If your hair is very dry from over processing you may find it more manageable by not rinsing the conditioner completely out.

Another alternative is to use a conditioner with silicone in it to further soften the hair and add more shine. If your hair is oily, use the conditioner only on the ends of the hair and rinse in cool water

LEAVE IN CONDITIONERS

If you are pushed for time or have flyaway frizzy hair, "leave in conditioners" could be a good option. There are many different forms of cremes on the market and it can be quite confusing.

If the ends of your hair are really dry you could use a leave in conditioner as a post styling fix to smooth frizzies and help hydrate and protect the ends. L'Oreal Intense Repair is perfect for defining curls and leaving the hair soft and free of frizz. Put a walnut size dab of creme into your hands and rub hands together, stroking it over and smoothing all sides of the length of the towel dried hair. Leave to dry naturally or dry with a diffuser.

If your hair is coarse or rough try L'Oreal Gliss Extreme in wet or dry hair. If it is chemically damaged or just super dry use Kevin Murphys Staying Alive (see „dandruff" for stockists)

As a rule it is best not to use too much product on your hair. Use NONE if you are going to a job, as the hair stylist will take care of your hair, depending on the specifics of what will be needed for that day. Nothing worse than having your hair washed again, when you get to the studio to get rid of your product.

SCALP TONICS

You may require a scalp tonic from time to time when your scalp gets out of condition. To check your scalp, make a parting in your hair and check for scaling, flaking or dryness. Some problems, such as dryness can be treated easily with a warm oil treatment.

Dandruff must be treated immediately with an appropriate treatment but don't rush to conclusions if you see flaking, sometimes it can be a build up of product or a result of sunburn. Dandruff commonly is accompanied by oily hair and is easily treated.

HAIR MASKS

You may like to use a hair mask once a week if your hair feels dry or damaged from heat styling, chemical processing or sun and salt exposure. To allow for a better absorption of the product, put a plastic disposable shower cap over your hair after applying the mask, and blast it with a warm hair dryer. Alternatively you can put on a hair mask before going into the sauna or at the beach. Follow the instructions on the product and always rinse thoroughly as product residue can easily lead to dull, lifeless hair.

DETOX SHAMPOOS

These shampoos have been specially created to strip the hair of styling preparations, chlorine and dirt. They contain higher concentration of detergents and chelators, which bind to the surface of the hair to remove collected minerals. Use a detox or clarifying shampoo when you feel you have had a heavy product using week/day in the studio. Lather up as per usual, but then leave on for a couple of minutes before rinsing and conditioning.

COMMON HAIR PROBLEMS

DANDRUFF You will need to make a scalp check to investigate signs of dandruff unless you have already noticed the tell tale signs on your shoulders. Dandruff normally appears in conjunction with oily or greasy patches that can easily become infected, resulting in scabbing and inflammation. This type of dandruff is normally linked with food allergies or a poor diet (sebhorric dermatitis) and is aggravated by stress or excessive intake of dairy products and junk foods.

Wash the hair daily with a shampoo specially formulated for dandruff. Alternatively, you can blend 10 drops of thyme essential oil with 100ml of apple juice, massage into scalp and leave on for 5 minutes, rinse the hair and then use a mild shampoo. (Use only high quality natural or organic products as artificially produced oils and juice will further aggravate the problem)

Take four 500mg capsules of evening primrose oil every day until the condition clears. Using an antidandruff shampoo may cause an accelerated fading in coloured hair. Best results can be achieved by using a shampoo that has exfoliating properties and works with AHA, an ingredient that works much the same way as a mild chemical peel. Kevin Murphys' Maxi Wash is good one to try (www.kevinmurphy.com.au)

England only – call: +44 012826613413 or check out web sites like www.hqhair.com Use the brand selector and currency converter.

FLAKY SCALP This condition can be confused with dandruff and can result from poor circulation, using harsh hair products, not rinsing shampoo out properly or not washing hair thoroughly. Use a mild shampoo and work it into the scalp thoroughly. If the scalp is not meticulously clean it can be a perfect breeding ground for bacteria. Shampooing will lift off dead skin cells but if not done thoroughly they will only flake off when the hair and scalp is dry. Avoid medicated shampoos as they can irritate the scalp.

ECZEMA If you find red patches that are itchy, it is likely you have eczema or psoriasis. If you are unsure ask a dermatologist or your hairdresser. Avoid medicated shampoos if you suspect you have eczema, as they can further irritate the scalp. Wash your hair daily with a mild or moisturizing shampoo and then massage a few drops of Aloe Vera juice or cold chamomile tea into the scalp and leave on over-night as a treatment. Rinse it out in the morning, as it can weigh the hair down, making it hard to handle. Try cutting out dairy food to see if it imroves.

TEMPORARY HAIR LOSS It is completely normal to lose 100 hairs each day. Temporary hair loss can also occur due to stress, taking medication or illness, the hair usually grows back. Deficiencies such as in zinc can cause hair loss and may be the cause of long term hair loss. A 20mg supplement of liquid zinc over an extended period (6months) will rectify the deficiency. (other symptoms can include lack of smell and taste)
Traction hair loss is caused by braiding or weaving hair tightly or too often and can cause scaring as it disrupts the hair follicle. Silica tissue salts can help the re-growth and slow the hair loss. Available at your local homeopathic.

FRIZZY HAIR Frizzy hair is caused by atmospheric moisture. Look for styling preparations that repel moisture like serums and pomades. Alternatively, try using a leave in conditioner after shampooing or adapt your hairstyle accordingly. In other words, encourage the natural movement of the hair, and don't fight against it! An ideal product to use is Kevin Murphys' Hair Screen. Apply it to towel dried hair, and let the hair dry naturally, accentuating the hairs natural movement. Born Again, another Kevin Murphy product, contains Omega 3 & 6 oils to moisturize and make wiry hair feel soft. (See dandruff for kevins web site)

STATIC HAIR Strands of hair have an electrical charge that is positive or negative. When either two positive or two negative hair strands repel each other, it makes the hair go static. This can come from the friction created when brushing your hair or from pulling an item of clothing over your head. Tame the hair with a spray of hair spray on your brush and brushing it through the hair or by using a hair product that has a moisturizing base to it as they restore the electrical balance to the hair

DULL HAIR This can result from a poor diet, bad circulation, a build up of styling products or harsh shampoos. To bring the shine back to your hair increase your intake of pantothenic acid, found in wheat germ, peanuts and egg yolks. A diet too low in essential fatty acids can affect the condition of your hair, scalp and skin. If your hair suddenly becomes dull and lifeless and the scalp is dry and flaky, check that your diet includes vegetable oils, nuts, seeds and oily fish such as sardines, red mullet and salmon. If you hate all of those include flaxseeds, crushed, at each meal and watch the shine return.
After shampooing, rinse your hair with a cupful of white wine or apple cider vinegar diluted with a litre of cold water. The acidity flattens the hair cuticles, making your hair shiny. Curly

hair can look dull, as the cuticles don't lie flat. Try a leave in conditioner or a non-greasy spray gloss avoiding the roots of the hair.

Many non-permanent hair colours, or rinses, as they are called, will create a beautiful shine by coating the hair and adding extra body to the hair. Clairol Nice'n easy for example, also has a great conditioner that accompanies the hair colour. Use one that is closest to your own hair colour if you have a special hair casting, and need that extra edge. DO NOT experiment with a new colour the day before an important casting. Most rinses say they wash out after about 8 washes, but the truth is they tend to last much longer especially on dry, porous hair. It is not recommended to use these products on bleached, highlighted or permed hair. Find a colour and brand you like the results of, and use it the day before the casting.

Safe alternatives for important castings or when you want to give your hair a shine booster try Aveda colored conditioners. Use one for your hair colour and leave it in for 20 minutes. This is a safe and great alternative to using a rinse, as it will pump up the colour and the shine in one go!

GROWTH

Hair has a growth rate of about 12mm a month and up to 15cm a year. You may find hair grows faster in warm, humid climates. Each strand has three growth phases before being replaced by a new hair. If not cut, hair will grow to about 107cm before being shed. Over time, growth decreases. To maintain a healthy hair growth, massage the scalp to ensure good circulation to the hair follicles and maintain a healthy diet that includes silicon rich foods such as oats, barley, spinach, asparagus, lettuce, tomatoes, cabbage, figs and strawberries.

MATTED OR TANGLED HAIR

Your hair should never become matted as you should be brushing it at least daily but if it does become excessively knotted, particularly at the base of the neck, from pullovers or scarves, try putting your scarf on the outside of your hair.

Hair should always be treated gently and never tugged at or stretched to snapping point. Start at the ends of your hair, slowly working through the hair up the hair shaft, to the roots. Work gently to avoid ripping the hair shaft. (Never tie wet hair up tightly as the hair expands as it dries and you may end up snapping hair off!)

Use a natural bristled brush and be patient. Daily thorough brushing of the hair stimulates hair growth, scalp circulation and distribution of hair oils, but more is not better.

If your hair has a lot of product from a job and seems impossible to detangle, do your best with a gentle brush, then wet your hair in the shower and apply a softening conditioner like Pantene Pro V. After applying the conditioner and squeezing it into the hair GENTLY start moving your fingers through the hair from the ends, like a giant comb. Once you are able to move your fingers easily through the hair in a combing action you can use a wide tooth comb to sort out the other tangles, again, moving from the bottom of your hair up and not tugging or ripping at your hair. You will get enough of that on the job! The best hair detangler is Born Again or Staying Alive by Kevin Murphy. Tangles will easily fall out leaving the hair soft and silky.

OVERTREATED HAIR

This is probably going to be everyone's problem sooner or later but let's hope you are one of the lucky ones who never has this problem!

If your hair has been bleached or highlighted and it feels like straw you can remedy the problem by using a softening conditioner such as Pantene Pro V smooth and silky. Apply it only on the length of your hair if it is normally fine or oily.

If your hair is really heavily bleached and feels like it might just snap off in your fingers, put a little conditioner in a spray bottle with water in it and after giving it a good shake to dissolve the conditioner, spray it onto the hair, massage it in so the hair feels like towel dried hair and blow dry as usual on a low heat setting.

If your hair has just been coloured over and over try a Pantene Pro V Mask in a sachet. Gliss Kur also has some good hair masks. Find one that is suitable for your condition and after applying it, put a disposable shower cap on over the mask and wrap your hair in a warm towel for a half an hour or so. Rinse well and finish with cold water to give the hair a good shine. Born Again by Kevin Murphy is also a wonder product for over treated hair and can turn a disaster back into hair. (for where to get Kevin Murphy products, see chapter on dandruff, page 30)

HAIR CUTS

If you are planning a drastic hair change or want to use your hairstyle to make the most of your features it is best to talk to your agency first and then to consult a hairdresser that you already know and trust. The following is a guideline of hair shapes designed to correct features that may be too prominent.

Fashion is very often an exaggeration of a particular look so remember to keep in mind what your client base is, and how you are perceived in the business. Very often a strong look may be ideal for an editorial market but the bread and butter clients such as catalogue and advertising may prefer a more conservative look, or one that is readily changeable, i.e.: hair length able to be put up as an alternative or swept back.

Doing something extreme to your hair either cut or colour wise can either start or ruin a career so contemplate the changes carefully and consult as many different sources as possible before taking the plunge.

Before you make any decisions, draw your hair back off your face and establish what your face shape is. You may have a combination of different shapes or cowlicks in the hairline.

(Cowlicks are the swirl of hair at scalp level that determines the direction of the hair growth and its anticipated projection) What is your natural hair texture and movement?

All these things must calculate into your end decision on a haircut, as there is no point deciding on a fringe if you have a cowlick right in the front of your hairline! Going WITH your natural hair tendencies is ALWAYS much more successful than fighting against them. The main aim is to take your natural mixture of texture, movement, length, cowlicks and face shape, to figure out which cut and style best suits you and your "look".

BANGS OR FRINGES   You can disguise a low / high hairline or an uneven hairline with a fringe. To draw attention away from thinning hair on the sides of the face, opt for a fringe that tapers down the sides of the temples. The longer the fringe, the wider the face will appear to be. A round face needs a short fringe to elongate it. Wide, broad fringes may make the eyes appear bigger but may also make the face seem wider. If you have a high forehead disguise it with a long fringe. If your forehead is low, choose a style with a wispy fringe, rather than a fuller one.

ROUND FACE   Height is needed at the crown to flatter a round face, and length overall, to help elongate the face. Styles that are not symmetrical tend to compliment this face shape so avoid scraping the hair severely back, centre parts, bobs and curly or flat styles. Feathered, layered or razor cut at the sides of the face, tend to soften and narrow the face and are therefore more complimentary to a round face.

SQUARE FACE   Angular faces tent to be emphasised by sharp jaw length cuts, heavy fringes and cuts cropped into the nape of the neck. Side partings, soft curls and other feminine styles that balance the proportions of the face will be more complimentary. Symmetrical shapes will emphasise the angular nature of the face.

LONG FACE   A fringe that is cut quite wide will give the illusion of width at the temples and a chin length cut will bring width at the lower part of the face. Avoid long straight styles and styles without fringes as these one length styles will emphasise the length of your face.

OVAL FACE   This is often considered the "ideal" face shape, as most hairstyles look good on this face shape. Most oval shaped faces do have a tendency to be wider at the forehead. This can be made less noticeable by cutting a fringe.

HEART SHAPED FACE   Height at the crown and width at the jaw line is the appropriate way to flatter a heart shaped face. Centre partings will only emphasise the point of the chin but off centre, feminine styles always suit this shape.

COMBINATION SHAPES   Chances are you will fall into a combination of shapes, such as round forehead with either a square jaw line or a combination of a long, square face. Either way, by reading what is recommended for both shapes, you can probably figure out what your hair strategy should be. The problem may really occur if you have a cowlick on your forehead hairline and you really want a fringe! Talk to your hairdresser about your alternatives and bring several pictures of the kind of haircuts you like with you.

PROMINENT FEATURES   If you have a prominent feature you would like to play down, here are some tips, but bare in mind that it could be the feature that makes you special in the mind of the clients. Ask your booker if she can tell you any of the comments she has heard the clients make about your look. You could be drawing the attention AWAY from your best asset!

A receding chin is not often a good asset so you can draw attention away from it by wearing your hair so the ends skim the sides of your chin. Slim down a broad neck by wearing your hair behind your ears, letting the hair fall around the neck. If you have a prominent nose a soft feminine style could be the most flattering.

CUTTING STYLES   Fine, flyaway hair can be cut in a short-layered style that will be easy to manage and create the illusion of body. Different lengths of layers should be incorporated into the cut. Thick and frizzy hair can be hard to manage and layering can make it even bigger and wilder. Instead, go for graduated layers around the base of the hair, which may help to weigh the hair down. Remember, sometimes going with what you naturally have been blessed with and even accentuating it, may be a way to create your own individual look.

HAIR STYLING

BLOW OUT   Before blow-drying your hair, prepare it by going through it with a wide tooth comb and getting rid of any tangles. Start at the end and don't rip, tear or pull at your hair. Apply a heat protecting spray evenly and lightly. Comb it through. Start off by rough drying the hair using your free hand to separate the hair and hold the dryer up high, always directing the air flow from the roots to the ends down the hair shaft to help close the cuticles and create a shine.

Always keep the hair dryer moving as you are working on the hair. The more styling your hair needs the damper it should be. If your hair is curly about 60% dry, if it is straight, about 80%. Now you are ready to style it.

Start on the under sections of the hair making sure that each section is completely dry before moving on to the next section. Don't use the hottest setting when you are working on the roots as this can irritate the scalp, making it greasy and flatten the hair.

Move the dryer in small rotations or use a gentle shaking motion, to keep the air moving and avoid overheating or burning the hair. Work your way up the head.

If you are using a brush to create curl or movement, wait until the hair is cool or blast it with cool air before removing the brush, otherwise the movement will drop out.

If you have limited time, start drying the hair around your face first and then work the top sections, leaving the underneath to dry naturally if the weather is permitting. It is often a good thing to let clients see your hair as it naturally is as they will see another side of how you can look without the styling you may have in your portfolio.

STRAIGHTENING IRON   Make sure your hair is completely dry before using the straightening iron. Work from the under section of the hair taking a small amount of hair and combing it with a fine toothed comb. When you are far enough down the hair shaft with the comb that the iron can fit between the comb and your roots, press the hair between the plates and start to move the comb and the iron simultaneously down the hair shaft, the iron chasing straight after the comb. The comb creates a smooth finish for the iron to press into place. Work your way up the head.

CURLING TONGS   The hair must be completely dry before starting to tong the hair. Begin with the under section of the hair, working your way up the head. Either wind the hair around the closed tong, holding the end of the hair close to the tong to create a loose and wild end or close the end of the hair in the beak of the tong and roll or wind the hair onto the tong, taking care not to burn yourself on the hot rod of the tong. You can either leave the hair to cool by itself for a softer movement or you can clip each curl up, into shape until it is cooled and then release the clip. The movement of the hair can be curled in the direction away from the face so as you walk, the wind can lift the hair out and up, away from your face. This creates a full and natural look to your hair and stops you fighting with it in your face all day.

STYLING PRODUCTS

Styling products should be restricted for use on your free days or when you are required to style yourself, for example castings and gosees.

If you are working you should always arrive in the studio or at the location with clean hair.

There are many different products to choose from so pay attention to your hair stylist and the products they use and how they use them, you could pick up some easy styling tips to use at home for yourself. Here are a few basic products and their uses, but there are an infinite amount of different products on the market, which can fit under the following headings.

SERUM   Usually silicone based, serums form a fine film on the surface of the hair shaft to bump up the hair shine and softness. Use sparingly, two or three drops rubbed into your hands and applied to wet hair to deal with tangles, or scrunch into curls to reduce frizz. On dry hair, smooth on down the shaft of the hair to give shine or use to temporarily seal split ends if they look dry and split. Try Aveda.

WAX   Used on short hair to add texture and definition to curly hair. To tame unruly hairs around the face and hairline, choose a light-weight formula. A heavier wax can be used for shorter styles or to break up thick hair.

Use sparingly by rubbing a small amount into the palms of your hands and either scrunching it into the hair or running the hands through the hair, avoiding the roots of the hair. For hairline control, put a small amount on your fingers and tame the hair directly. Baby hair around the hairline can be either smoothed into the rest of the hair or smoothed down to create a feature, as long as it doesn't leave a "bald patch" where it meets the longer hair.

GEL   Available in different consistencies ranging from sprays to thicker jelly types. Use on wet hair to set the hair into a wet style look or add to the roots before blow-drying for extra hold and volume. Use on dry hair to slick it down or on shorter hair to add texture. If the gel dries and feels brittle, add a small amount of serum to the gel before applying.

HAIR SPRAY   Use hair spray as a finishing preparation to keep hair in place unless it is likely you will be rained on. Hair spray and water do not mix. To smooth stray hairs, spray directly onto your brush or comb and brush through hair to control flyaway and static.

SETTING LOTION   There are an infinite variety of products that can come under this heading and they have an array of different funky names but they are all essentially going to coat the hair and add body. They usually contain flexible resins that form a film on the hair to help when styling and prevent heat damage. They can be added to the roots to create lift and lightly to the lengths of the hair to create body and shine. (Unless the product specifically states that it has a matting effect.)

These products are a great alternative to gel. They are lighter and won't easily weigh down the hair. Overloading the hair can happen, causing the hair to feel stiff and tangled, so go easy and remember with some products, less is

more and even less, can be perfect.

CREAM   Adding shine, light hold and moisture, creams are a great solution to frizzy slightly curly hair or straight fine hair. Use cremes sparingly on dry hair to smooth down the shaft of the hair, creating shine and a polished look. Rubbing a hazelnut size amount of cream between your hands, move the palms of your hands very lightly over the surface of smooth hair catching only the "frizzy" parts. Slowly distribute the rest of the cream through the ends of the hair by combing your fingers through the hair to add texture. Start lightly and avoid the roots, you are always able to add more later if you feel it is necessary. These products should be seen as a light dressing or polish to long straight hair or fine hair and added more liberally to curly, dryer hair types.

FOAM   Also available in a wide range of types, foams are generally used to add volume and root lift to fine or limp hair. With current fashion having less emphasis on volume and more on the natural health and movement of the hair, there are many alternatives that may work more efficiently and are easier to get right. Foams should be rubbed between your two hands and applied to wet hair at the roots. This will create hold and lift from the roots when blow-drying, without making the length of the hair immobile from product.

SPECIAL PRODUCTS

Some products on the market don't really fall into some of these broad terms for hair products and I just want to mention a couple of my favorites, you might like to try on your days off. Kevin Murphy (see end of dandruff chapter for details) has a product called Hair Screen. Great for that beach hair look. Apply it to dry hair. Another favorite is Sticky Business. Also apply to dry hair in a scrunching fashion, to create volume, texture and that just slept in look!

TOOLS

HAIR DRYER   Probably the most common hair tool, the hair dryer is one of the most versatile tools. Choose a dryer that has at least 2 or 3 heat settings and 2 speeds. Dryers that have around 1800 watts are going to give you a faster and more professional blow dry, even if you were a bit sloppier with the brush. The nozzle that comes with the dryer is not an accessory, it controls the airflow and will direct it down the shaft of the hair, creating a smooth shiny finish.

STRAIGHTENING IRON   These can be quite varied but it is always advised to use a heat protecting styling spray first on the hair, as only the high-end ceramic versions can control their heat according to the hair requirements. It is highly recommended not to use straightening irons daily, only intermittently, and NEVER on wet, damp or highly processed hair. Cordless versions are now available which makes handling of the irons easier and smaller ceramic versions are even easier still.

CRIMPERS   These tools are basically the same idea as straighteners, and the same rules apply except they press the hair into ripples or waves. They often come with interchangeable attachments to create different sized waves. Avoid these tools altogether if you have bleached, very dry or otherwise highly processed hair, as they have a tendency to dry out the hair which could lead to breakage.

HEATED ROLLERS   Hot rollers can be a quick and simple way to restyle hair and can be found in a variety of forms from hot/electric papilloten or hot sticks, to "steam" activated rollers. As a general rule hot rollers should never be used on wet hair unless otherwise stated by the manufacturer. There are a variety of ways to roll the hair. The angle and direction in which the hair is rolled, will result in root lift and which direction the hair will fall, when the hair is cool and released from the roller. It is important to wait for the hair to be completely cool before releasing the roller from the hair so as to lock the curl in, preventing the curl from dropping.

TONGS   These are a great tool for creating movement and curl at high speed. Available in a variety of barrel sizes, depending on the size of curl you want to create. The same rules as straightening irons apply, not to be used on wet, damp or bleached hair. They are a little more difficult to use, so be extra careful around ears, face and when you are getting closer to the scalp. To clean tongs, wipe over with a damp cloth or use mentholated spirits when they are completely cool and unplugged.

HAIR UPKEEP

CLEANSING   Either choose a shampoo that is suited to your hair type, or invest in a very mild formulation, as you will be washing your hair more often than most people. You should always come to the studio with washed, clean hair, unless the hair stylist requests something otherwise.

If your mild shampoo doesn't lather into a mass of suds and bubbles, this doesn't mean it won't clean your hair thoroughly. In fact, as the amount of suds is determined by the active level of detergent in the product, one that is milder may be more effective for this very reason.

Don't ever wash your hair with dish washing liquid or other detergents as they are very alkaline and may disrupt the PH balance of your scalp .

Don't rinse your hair in your bath water, as a soapy residue will always remain, causing the hair to be dull and lifeless when dry.

If you wash your hair daily, one shampoo and rinse should suffice. Concentrate, when washing your hair, on the top of the head (open hand-span directly on top of the head) and around the oil gland areas behind the ears (when you put your thumbs in your ears, the area your fingers reach behind your ears) This is where the hair is likely to be the oiliest and a breeding ground for bacteria.

Keep the water temperature tepid when you are washing your hair, as hot water can agitate the scalp and stimulate the activity of the oil glands, making hair greasy and flat. Before applying the conditioner squeeze as much excess water out of your hair as possible.

CONDITIONING If you skip using your conditioner, it can result in the cuticles of your hair shaft not lying flat. Your hair will look dull and lifeless. Conditioners play a major role in maintaining the shine and the general appearance of the hair. There are many conditioners to choose from so invest in one specifically for your hair type and needs. Apply the conditioner only to the lengths of the hair, as the scalp will quickly supply the hair with the sufficient moisture from the oil glands. After applying and squeezing through the hair length, run your fingers through the hair to distribute. Even with long hair, as long as you can easily drag your fingers through the hair, the conditioner will be distributed.

Leave in your hair for between 1-3 minutes depending on the instructions, then gently rinse thoroughly and finish with a blast of cold water. This will make sure the cuticles will lie flat and stimulates the blood flow to the scalp, encouraging all the nutrients for healthy hair growth.

MASKS You will have to use your own judgement when deciding how often to use a mask, but remember; one of the main causes of lifeless looking hair, is over-conditioning. Use a deep conditioning mask if your hair is dry and damaged from chemical processing, excessive heat styling or sun and salt water exposure.

Protein masks rebuild the hair, as they are absorbed into the cuticle. They strengthen the hair shaft. Moisturizing packs help to hydrate and improve manageability. Use a mask on freshly washed hair that has been blotted with a towel to remove excess water. Don't rub your head with the towel as the cuticles are open and the hair shafts will become entangled and matted easily. To increase the effect and absorption of the mask, apply before going into a sauna or steam room. (as mentioned in Hair Masks) Before going to the beach lather on a hair mask to let the sun activate the ingredients but never sleep with a hair mask on, you could wake up with it all over!

CARE

Having your hair regularly trimmed will not only keep the shape of your hair style but will keep your hair in good condition as any damaged, split ends will be cut off, but there are some ways to keep the damage to a minimum. How you treat your hair daily will pay off even if it occasionally gets tortured at work in the studio. Pay attention to how your hair responds to the products that get used on you and those you use at home. Get to know your hair and recognise the signs of when it needs a little more moisture or replenishing. Both of these terms are used to discribe products in the hair care industry that will help to give back some silkiness to dry or damaged hair, leaving it less prone to being frizzy. If your hair is dry and damaged avoid products that offer volume or body as the key for you is moisturizing. Avoid products that will dry your hair out like sodium lauryl sulphate or hairsrays and hair gels, as they contain alcohol. When washing your hair don't pile long hair on top of your head and bunch it all up. Gently massage the scalp with your fingers and let the shampoo rinse through the length of the hair to freshen it up. Keep your conditioner concentrated at the ends of your hair and eat plenty of good quality protein and drink water!

NAILS

It is the responsibility of the professional model to keep his or her nails impeccable.

Both hands AND feet should always be freshly manicured and pedicured. It is your choice to have them varnished or not, but use pale, neutral or French polish colours.

As it is not always convenient to find a nail parlour if you are travelling a lot. It is best, and professional, to be able to do your own nails so they are always kept in good condition. Clients notice if your hands are well groomed. This could be another selling point in your favour.

A client may be wavering as to whom to choose for a job, but a model with all good points will definitely have the edge. If the picture only requires a fleeting hand shot, someone with well-groomed hands will seem more attractive for the client to book.

If you think your hands and nails are too ugly anyway...read on.

TOOLS

A Loose cotton wool
B Wooden orange stick
C Cuticle clippers
D Nail scissors
E Nail cleaning implement or „knife"
F Nail buffer
G Nail grader
H Emery board
I Cuticle remover creme
J Hand creme
K Nail polish
L Nail polish remover
M Pumice stone

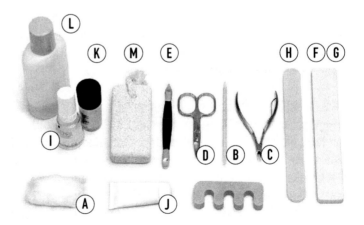

Even if you do not have the most beautiful nails or hands it is possible to improve the shape and appearance of the nails with regular attention.

A regular manicure and pedicure increases blood circulation and therefore nutrition to the nails. Just as important to the appearance of the nails, it trains the nails. The regular, gentle pushing back of the cuticles allows the nail bed to elongate and have a better shape.

This, in turn, instantly makes the nails look longer, even when the nail is not growing far over the tip of the finger. It makes the fingers look longer and more elegant. If you think it sounds like too much time and hard work, try doing it while watching TV. You can still hear the television and it only takes a second to look up to catch the action. You can utilize the time doing something productive, instead of having the time be unproductive. It is the perfect time to do your nails, as you must wait for the nails to dry between coats and after painting them. What better excuse do you need to stay put on the sofa than with wet nails?

Sometimes nails can develop white flecks on the surface of the nail. This is commonly found where there is a deficiency in zinc. Take a zinc supplement of around 20mg per day if you are deficient. Zinc plays an important role in the proper function of the immune system as well as being related to hair loss and cell growth so be sure you regularly eat your pumpkin seeds hummus and oysters. All great sources of zinc!

Keep hang nails (those small pieces of nail or skin that catch on fabrics) trimmed right at the root, so they do not catch and tear. Keep your nails a uniform length, which means if one breaks, you should cut them all so they all look uniform in length. I know this may break some hearts but it looks unattractive if one nail is much shorter than the others. It is better to have them all short and perfectly shaped than all different lengths.

MANICURE

1. Remove old varnish completely before starting a manicure. If the varnish is thick or a very strong colour, hold the cotton wad with the remover on it firmly, in the middle of the nail for a few seconds, before wiping down the length of the nail.

Try to remove all traces of varnish with several cotton wool pads as needed. Never over saturate the cotton wool, as the nail varnish will dissolve and the colour will run under the nail and be difficult to remove.

2. Dip the pointed end of an orange stick into a glass of water. Take a small wad of loose cotton wool and using the wet end of the stick, wrap the cotton wool firmly around the tip.

3. To secure the cotton wool, simply twist the wet stick and simultaneously hold the cotton wool in place. The water will make the cotton adhere to the orange stick.

4. The cotton tipped orange stick can be inserted carefully into the varnish remover and used to clean away any last traces of old varnish stuck by the cuticle, or under the nail.

5. Using cuticle cream to soften the skin around the nails, roughly rub in a small amount around the nail.

6. Soak the nails if you are not yet into a regular routine with your nails. Soaking them will soften any hard skin and make the cuticle and nail softer and easier to remove. Always soak the feet if you are doing a pedicure or do the feet straight after a long shower or bath.

7. When drying the hands, gently push the cuticle back towards the knuckles as you go, to remove the water and crème.

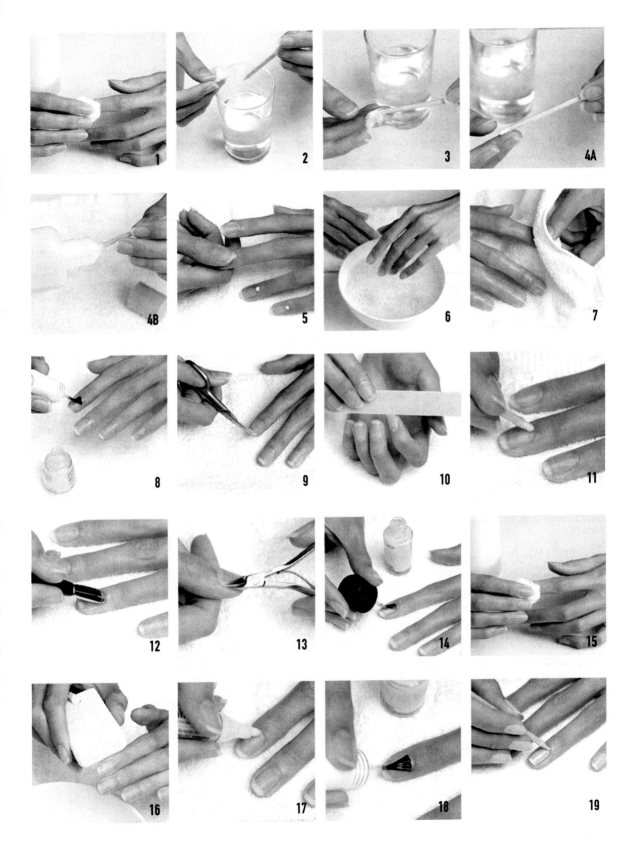

8. Apply cuticle remover with a brush and push the remover up into the cuticles with the end of the brush.

9. Keep your nails trimmed to a moderate length to be practical, attractive and contemporary. An oval or slightly squarish shape is the best to keep the nail strong and attractive. Pointy nails should be avoided.

10. File your nails from the outside edge, towards the centre and DO NOT use a seesaw motion. A back and forwards movement will encourage the layers of the nails to separate and therefore increase splitting of the nails. The shape of the nail should imitate the tip of the finger.

11. Again, dip your orange stick into water and wrap a small wad of cotton wool around the pointed tip to now remove the dead cuticle. Make the wad of wool slightly bigger than what you used for the remover. Using a circular motion, starting in the middle of the cuticle area, work the cotton wool in small circles rotating outwardly. The idea is not to go against any hangnails or cut skin so as to discourage hangnails and split skin that can catch on fabrics and tear at the skin.

12. Should you find it helpful, you may also use a cuticle knife to push back and gently lift the cuticle away from the nail surface.

13. Use the cuticle clippers to remove hangnails from their very root. Try to avoid cutting the cuticles themselves unless they are very long and unattractive. Be very careful to avoid cutting into the cuticle as raggedy edges will catch on fine fabrics and will tear the skin which could cause the skin to bleed. Always cut the cuticle smoothly and only when absolutely unavoidable.

14. Let the nails dry for a few minutes if you have been soaking them in water. When the nails are too moist, the varnish may bubble, spoiling your concentrated work. Use a base coat to avoid any stain a strong colour may leave behind. Usually two light coats are sufficient for most colours. Unless specific colours are requested or used on a job, keep your nails neutral and natural looking.

15. Squeak nails with a cotton wool pad and remover before applying your varnish to ensure the nail is free of oil. This will help to avoid the peeling of the nail varnish. (allow the nail surface to dry before painting)

16. A pumice stone may be used gently on thick or rough skin after soaking.

17. Between manicures, cuticle oils and moisturizers may be used to keep the skin soft and moist.

18. When painting the nails, gently press on the brush to fan the bristles out and flatten the brush. This technique will allow you to get close to the cuticle, achieve an accurate shape and cover a large area of the nail surface. With practice you will soon be able to quickly paint your nails with 3 strokes of the brush. When done quickly the edges of each stroke run into each other forming an even, beautiful finish. Use sheer, pale colours to start with.

19. If you should accidentally drown the cuticle or get varnish on the skin use your wet orange stick trick with just a whisk of cotton wool. Dip the wool tip quickly in some remover and carefully remove the excess varnish to achieve a flawless finish!

PEDICURE

A pedicure is basically the same as a manicure except you may need to soak the feet longer in the water. The skin and cuticles around the toe nails can be very dry and tough to remove, as feet tend to be quite neglected.

Toenails can also be trained by regular pedicures, to be much more regular looking and attractive. If you are having mild trouble with ingrown toenails, cutting a V shape into the nail will help take the pressure off the nail corner. Cut the v shape directly into the nail on the side of the nail which has the ingrown problem but not really close to the corner of the nail.

After soaking the feet you may need to use a pumice stone to remove the dry thick skin on the feet. It is very important to take care of this thick skin not only because it looks and feels unsightly and rough but because if the skin becomes too thick it can feel as if you are walking on a stone in your shoe.

The skin is easily removed when it is soft from soaking the feet, or if the skin is really tough, try doing it when you have had a long warm bath. Pumice stones are cheap and found in drug stores, chemist shops and The Body Shop. NEVER use any kind of cutting devise such as a razor or scissors!! Some shops sell a tool that looks a bit like a fine cheese grater and is for the feet, but a pumice stone will leave a smooth surface and can also be used on elbows, side of toes or fingers where necessary.

Toenails should always be neatly trimmed and kept short. The shape of the nail is generally straighter across than the finger nails because of the danger of ingrown nails, but be careful the nails are not sharp on the edges because they can press into the neighbouring toes when tightly pressed into shoes.

Always keep your toenails neatly trimmed as they are often showing due to undressing and wearing open toed shoes and sandals on jobs. Even if your feet are not the main thing in the picture, others notice and you will feel more beautiful if you can be proud of your toenails. Remember, they can be trained to be beautiful with regular attention.

Initially it may take a weekly pedicure if you are looking for some major improvements, but a monthly or three weekly pedicure should be your routine. Varnish on the toes usually stays quite well but avoid bright or strong colours as they will be obvious on a job and these colours are hard to remove when in a hurry. Try to stay with a neutral sheer pale pink, such as Macs' "Pretty Miss" or a French polish. (White varnish on the tip and covered with sheer pink)

VARNISH

When choosing a varnish which you intend to keep on for your next job always choose a low key, natural tone such as the above mentioned colours.

After allowing your nails time to dry, start with your thumb and push down slightly on the brush as you slide it up close to the cuticle. This will spread the fibres of the brush and allow you to get right up close to the cuticle without touching it. Stroke the brush downwards towards the end of the nail and start immediately with the next stroke.

By keeping the strokes coming in quick succession the varnish doesn't dry too quickly, allowing the edges of the different strokes to run together in a seamless coat of polish. Start on one side of the nail, then the middle then the last side. Aim for only 3 strokes per nail, as the more you stroke the brush and the varnish across the nail, the thicker and more irregular the varnish becomes. Move on to the pointer finger and so on, until it is time for the second hand. If you are not used to painting your nails, you may want to wait a few minutes until the first hand is dry so as not to smudge your hard work. The reason you should start with the thumb is because it is easier not to smudge the other fingers if you move from the thumb first and then to the pointer finger and so on.

Leave your first coat to dry well before applying a second coat otherwise the varnish will be dry to the touch, but will stay soft for ages afterwards, increasing the risk of damaging when later trying to find something in your purse etc. When doing the second coat you should be a little lighter with the brush, have a little more varnish on the brush and try to be slightly faster with your strokes. The first coat is meant for accuracy, the second coat is all about a light touch and a bit quicker.

If you find you have hit the edges with the varnish and unfortunately drowned the cuticle with polish, take heart. You can use the pointy end of the orange stick to clean up a few indiscretions, but if it is really all over the skin use a really tiny bit of cotton wool wrapped around the orange stick, dipped in varnish remover to do a little cleaning up.

If you really don't have time to make them perfect, polish that is on the skin or cuticles can be coaxed off in the shower. As the skin swells from the water, the varnish doesn't stretch with it, so you can easily scratch it off. Take care not to damage the cuticle skin as it will also be soft in the shower or bath and could be easily damaged by scratching at it too hard.

It is hard to keep nails looking great in big cities such as London, Paris or New York as the filth of the city gets into every little corner of you. You will notice when you blow your nose how black it is, well that grime gets stuck in your nails too so try to wash your hands at every chance you get to stop the grime from inbedding in your cuticles and nails. Use a nail brush to really get them clean! Moisturize dry cuticles to protect them from the grime.

QUICK MANICURE

The quick manicure is intended for those who have already worked on the nails enough to have them looking good. In other words the cuticles are back as far as they will go and are well lifted off the nail bed. There is no skin stuck to the nail close to the cuticle. There are no hangnails and rough, dry skin around the nails but varnish is old and the nails need to be in tiptop condition.

Remove the old varnish thoroughly with cotton wool and the cotton tipped orange stick dipped in varnish remover. Swipe the nails quickly around the cuticle with the cuticle remover brush. Where there is any dry skin on the sides of the nail add a little extra cuticle remover. Wait 3 minutes for the cuticle remover to soften the skin and do its job. With fresh cotton wool on the orange stick, rub in a clockwise and counter clockwise direction around the cuticle, to rub away any dead skin. Wipe any leftover cuticle remover off with a wad of cotton wool and use the reverse side of the wool to squeak the nails with varnish remover. Vigorously shake the nail varnish you intend to use and paint your first coat on carefully. Wait at least 10 minutes and then do another thin quick coat. Wait a good 15 minutes before doing anything to endanger the fresh varnish getting damaged.

After the nail varnish is completely dry, apply a really good hand moisturizer. If you are on the go a good one for your handbag is Muji handcreme as it smells fresh and soaks in to give you a greaseless finish (it does take at least 5 minutes) The best one of all, which is greasy so is only good when you have plenty of time to let it soak in and do its job, is the body shops' cocoa butter moisturizer in the tub. Try vanilla bean or almond and lather it on while watching TV for the silkiest hands and cuticles in town.

SELF TANNERS

Self-tanning is best done out of a bottle or in moderation in sun beds or if time permits, in conjunction with a sunscreen, in the sun.

If you have had any kind of cosmetic peel in the last 12 months or are using a moisturizer with AHAS, a sun block should be used on the face, (30+) and a fake tan, to match the colour of the face to the body. You may in fact get enough sun from your trips but remember to use the appropriate sun protection for your skin type.

There are many different self-tanning products to choose from but they all require some buffing or rubbing to achieve an even colour. Sprays are easier to apply but will also need some rubbing in and strategic avoidance of areas such as elbows, knees and heels to make the tan look believable. Gradual tanning moisturizers are less tricky and can be applied to knees and armpits occasionally. Try Dove or Boots brands. Avoid an orange or yellow colour and build the colour up over a few applications to achieve an even glow. This is not a body building competition; clients will be looking for nothing more than a healthy glow.

The moment someone asks you where you have been on holiday, you know you are over the tanning limit, so hold off on the bottle for a few weeks. Skin brushing makes a fake tan smoother and more even but drop it back to 3 times a week if you are using a fake tan. If you are regularly swimming in the ocean you may not need to skin brush at all.

Some self-tanners will stain clothing or bed sheets so find a time for application when you can do something else while you wait for it to fully dry. (Without freaking out your flatmate)

As mentioned, use a body skin brush on dry skin to first remove the dead skin, then shower using a mild body wash such as Eucerine Body Wash Gel. Towel yourself dry and if you have very dry elbows knees and heels you can firstly lightly moisturize them with your regular moisturizer.

Start with your legs and whether you use a spray or creme, buff and rub it in with your hands. (Thin, rubber medical type gloves can be used) The residue that is on your hands should be enough to sweep over your knees and elbows lightly. Pay special attention to areas that usually are a little darker when you naturally tan in the sun, such as the top of your thighs and the outside of your calves.

Move next to your butt and stomach. Remember stomachs tend to go quite brown and when doing your butt, bend over slightly so you get a smooth transition of colour from your legs onto your butt cheeks. Don't forget to pay special attention to the inside leg and the back of legs so no white GT stripes spoil your hard work! Move up to the small of your back and sides of your torso. Do the best you can with your back area, start with going from the waist up and then over the shoulders. Getting a friend to help with your back or leaving it out completely is better than doing a bad job and leaving streaks and white patches. If it needs to be in the picture, the makeup artist will darken it to match the other colour, but it will be more difficult if you haven't faded the colour in, or if the colour is really irregular.

Finish off with your breasts, chest and arms. Again, just skim over your elbows with the residue on your hands and fade the colour up onto your neck. Arms and shoulders tend to be quite brown but be careful with your hands, as brown knuckles can look really obvious. Skim over them as you did with elbows and knees.

If you are using a separate type of fake tan for your face, wash your hands and move to the different product. You will only use the tips of your fingers for the face and it will be easier to re-wash your hands the second time. Pay particular attention to your hairline, edges of eyebrows, ears, neck and jaw line. Use the residue on your fingers to smooth over the brow bone and moustache area, as these should be slightly lighter anyway.

Wash your hands immediately, paying special attention to the palms and in-between fingers and the dryer skin around your nails. Use a soft nail brush loaded with bar soap (wet the brush and rub the bristles of the brush into the soap, until you get a build up of soap on the bristles of the brush) Scrub your palms, in between fingers and the nails thoroughly, then rinse your hands underwater to get the soap off but don't let the water concentrate too much on the top of your hands where you have just put the tanner. Pat your palms dry.

Easiest, cheapest and most effective are the slow build up tanning moisturizers. They are a fool proof way of builing up a natural glow without streaks, but they do stain your hands.

FACIAL AND BODY HAIR

As a professional model it is important for you to be attentive to any small factor that could influence a client not to book you. Facial hair for women, especially those that regularly do beauty or close up work, is something that must be looked at with the greatest scrutiny. Some countries such as the USA, can be much less tolerant of even forearm hair, let alone top lip hair, so check with your booker (or close friend) if you are uncertain. Lip waxes are recommended to be done a week before a close up or beauty job, if you have the luxury of advance notice. Wax that does not feel too hot for the lip may still be too hot for the rarely waxed skin and can cause small pimples. The redness is known to last days so don't wax your lip the day before a job. Ask your beautician to use a wax for sensitive skins and to check for very fine hairs as these may show up in strong photographic light especially for closeup beauty work.

It may be necessary for some light haired women to wax the sides of the face if they have a lot of fine hair that would be noticed on a close up. This facial hair can be hereditary or the result of a hormonal imbalance and we all have it, it is just more noticeable on some than others. (If the condition is severe contact your doctor / dermatologist and have a blood test to detect possible hormonal imbalances and receive treatment.)

Waxing will remove the hair for up to six weeks or more. Permanent methods can be used such as lazers and electrolysis if the hair is somewhat coarse. For fine hair, waxing is the only reasonable method.

Bikini lines, legs and armpits should, as a rule, always be attended to as a model. You are often changing your clothes in front of others and some garments are more see through than others so keep your bikini line, underarms and legs smooth and hairless. This should be part of your grooming routine. It is not necessary to shave your legs daily but underarms should not have stubble of any length, at any time. Lingerie models will have to choose whether waxing or shaving is more suitable for them. Hot waxing at home is not recommended for the novice. It can be messy and potentially dangerous. Waxing can be quickly and expertly performed for a small fee by a beauty professional, so don't waste your time or money doing this at home.

Nipple hairs can rarely be seen and, if preferred, be simply tweezed out.

A lot of men choose to shave chest hair but hair on the back should be waxed, as it is quite difficult to get to alone and the back is not a particularly sensitive area. If you choose to shave chest hair, prepare the hair by first trimming it with hair clippers or scissors. The following instructions are also applicable for women who shave their legs.

Have a warm shower or bath to open the hair follicle. The warm water will also warm and soften the hair. Using a shaving gel for sensitive skin, lather the chest or legs well. Use a new disposable twin blade shaver, (not the shaver you normally use for your face if you are a man).

It is important not to risk infection or razor burn, as retouching hundreds of red spots can be a nightmare for a makeup artist or client, so keep shavers immaculately clean and regularly replaced. If you get goose bumps while shaving, stop shaving immediately as you will cut the tops off the bumps and end up a spotty, bleeding mess that will look aweful in a picture!

Legs should be shaved going against the direction of the hair growth to create a smooth finish but underarms or chests can have several different growth directions, so feel how smooth the surface is with your free hand.

After shaving apply Aloe Vera to the freshly shaved area to help heal the surface of the skin of any minor nicks or scratches. Aloe Vera can also be used to soothe and heal the skin

directly after waxing or plucking. If you choose to shave in the shower (especially for legs) be careful not to continue shaving if you have goose pimples as this will also result in a lot of red dots that will take a few days to heal. If you do take the tops off the goose pimples with the razor, apply Aloe Vera and be careful to NEVER DO IT AGAIN!

Ingrown hairs can be annoying as well as painful and unsightly. If you are prone to ingrown hairs be sure to include dry skin brushing to slough off dead skin and stimulate blood supply.

An inexpensive product is available at the chemist called magnesium sulphate paste. A small amount can be gently heated on a piece of aluminium foil using a lighter under the foil. We are not talking about cooking the magnesium paste, just gently warming it so it is comfortable to put on the ingrown hair. The paste has a drawing quality and will help to draw the hair out. Follow by using Aloe Vera to soothe the area.

Never try to pick the hair out with a needle or blade. Ask your beautician to advise, and help you as she is used to such situations and will keep the health of your skin in mind.

PLUCKING EYEBROWS

Using the line from the outside corner of your nose to the inside corner of the eye, draw an imaginary line (or hold up a pencil or brush) and use this point as the guide to where the brow should start. Make the edge of the two brows soft, so it looks natural and keep the brows an even and harmonious thickness all the way through. Avoid tadpole or angular shapes.

Brows should be plucked to create as much height as possible between the eye and the eyebrow, so only take hairs from below the brow, to help create height. Extreme shapes (too thin or angular) will make the face look hard or artificial so take care not to over pluck and keep to the most natural shape possible.

DIET

Your diet is an important part of your job, as **staying trim** and **looking beautiful** is one of the **main expectations** people have of a model.

Without going into explanations of anatomy, physiology and nutrition, it is necessary for you to understand what foods to eat and when, so you are able to follow a long term eating plan that will supply you with the energy you need for your busy days and most importantly, that will supply you with all the vitamins, minerals and fats you need to stay looking good. As models, you have specific requirements from your diet such as keeping you slim and beautiful but also that can be easily adapted when you are on a job abroad in an exotic location or are trying to save money when in places such as London and Paris. There are many books on the subject and countless diets that guarantee fast weight loss, but the basic facts are as follows: All food you eat is fuel for the body. When you are not burning the fuel at the same rate that you are supplying the fuel, the body will store the fuel as energy for harder times.

Some foods are better at supplying the body with the nutrients it requires and therefore are superior in quality than others.

As you know by now, quality is always better than quantity, and your body needs a balance of high quality foods to function well.

Your body needs fibre, water, vitamins & minerals, fats and proteins. The best sources of all these things are found in pure foods. This means, as little processing as possible. Fruits and vegetables are fibre foods supplying an amazing array of vitamins and minerals as well as pure water. Fats and proteins are found in seeds, legumes, nuts, lean meat and tofu.

In all countries of the world you will be able to find cheap, easy to prepare foods of this kind in abundance. As being relatively cheap they are the best foods for you to consider as the main part of your diet. You may wonder what role fats play in the diet of a model. They are essential for keeping your skin and hair smooth and shiny as well as controlling your hunger and weight, so be sure to include only the best quality sources otherwise you will not be getting the value fats supply, and they will only make you gain weight. Natural fats found in seeds, nuts and avocados are the best to help control cravings and hunger pangs.

As a rule try to have as little sugar as possible in your diet and restrict your sugars to only the natural kind. The reason for this is that sugars supply a lot of energy, or fuel and unless you intend to burn them all off at the gym, it is best to have sugars that contain a lot of fibre, like fruit so the sugar is released slowly as energy.

Keep the fibre and water in your diet as high as possible, as you will avoid bloating and fluid retention. High fibre foods such as salad and vegetables are necessary for regular bowel movements and will contribute to your digestive health. Constipation can make you feel bloated, fat and in a really bad mood, so it is best to be avoided at all costs. If you have problems with bloating, drink Nettle tea, and stay away from foods with MSG (monosodiumglutimate) as it can make you retain fluid and cause headaches and food cravings.

Poor sources of proteins contain bad fats, which is why it is best to eat only good quality proteins such as fish, tofu, nuts, seeds, legumes and sprouts. These will supply you with good amounts of protein as well as the right kinds of fats for energy and the essential amino acids. They will make you feel satisfied for long periods. Even if it is just a snack of 6 nuts and an apple it will keep you satisfied for a couple of hours. Supplement your diet with essential fatty acids (Omega 3's) which will help you metabolise fats and help you with controlling weight and hunger.

The best rule of thumb is to have a breakfast that supplies you with good quality, slow burning energy to take you through the first half of the day. A lunch that consists of plenty of fibre and slow burning energy, and a dinner that is on the lowest level of high energy food as you will not have time to burn it off in the evening. Drinking a glass of water every hour is the only way to be sure you get enough water throughout the day. You will not get the benefits from the water for your skin and digestion if you drink one litre in one sitting. Especially important is not to drink large quantities of water with food, as this will dilute the digestive juices needed to breakdown your food. The best is to have small increments of water throughout the day.

GROCERY SHOPPING

Grocery shopping can be fun, especially in a foreign country so enjoy the experience and take your experience as an adventure.

Bring a small dictionary with you if you must, but all the foods you need, will be obvious to you and you will just need to smell and squeeze them the same as you do at home.

Allow more time to wander and investigate different things in a supermarket but outdoor markets will be full of sellers who will be helpful to you. In France for example, the labels of the foods in supermarkets are more beautiful so take note of how things look different and you will gain an insight into how different cultures appreciate other aesthetics. You will still find the yoghurt in the cooled cabinets!

When choosing fruits and vegetables smell and touch is important but use your sight too as some sellers don't want people squeezing their produce without buying.

FRUITS When buying fruits note the following: Only buy the freshest and best quality fruits. If you can afford it, and they are available to you, buy organic, as they are grown without the use of chemicals or pesticides and will be better for you. As organic produce becomes more and more in demand, the prices will eventually become more competitive.

Strawberries should be eaten in season and should have a strong strawberry smell, even if they are wrapped. Pick them up and smell close to any opening of the wrapper. If you can't smell them don't buy them, as they will also have no taste. Try this in Italy, the smell is really strong.

Rock melons or cantaloupe should also have a distinct melony smell when they are ripe. Put your nose to the part where the melon was attached to the vine. If you don't smell the delicious smell of the melon then don't buy it.

Blueberries should be organic where possible. They should be firm and a dark blue colour with no wrinkly skin or discolour.

Lemons should be firm and heavy as the ones containing the most juice will be the heaviest.

Tomatoes should be firm but give a little as you squeeze. Try to buy the ones with the part of the vine still attached, as they will be as fresh as the vine showing looks.

Avocadoes should be slightly yielding to a squeeze and should not have black areas on the skin. If you can't get ripe ones, buy the hard ones and put them in a paper bag outside the fridge for a day until they ripen.

VEGETABLES Vegetables should make up the bulk of your diet and a wide variety should be eaten. Try to eat those vegetables that are in season and look the best when you are in the market. Wash them thoroughly and rub the skin with your hands. The ones that should always be a part of your regular menus are the following:

Broccoli should be firm (no wobbly stalk) and the floret or top part should be dark green and free from yellow or brown parts that have gone to seed. Broccoli that has gone to seed tastes bitter and unappetizing. Broccoli doesn't have a particularly long shelf life (even though you keep it in the refrigerator) Try to cook it within the first 2 days. Steaming or boiling are the best alternatives to raw, but try to eat at least a handful of raw broccoli every week. Broccoli is done when a sharp knife is easily put into the stalk when cooking. It should be still slightly crunchy and bright green. (see broccoli soup pg.118)

Cucumbers should be firm and not rubbery. Eat them with the skin on for added fibre. Serve sliced thinly with yogurt and dill or in salad.

Green Beans should also be firm and fat, not withering at the ends. Cook them quickly in boiling water so they are bright green and crunchy or add them to a quick stir fry.

Zucchini or Courgettes should be firm to the touch and come in dark and light green. They should be steamed or poached lightly in a stir-fry and taste sweet when cooked properly.

Bell Peppers (also called Capsicum or Paprika) should be firm and have smooth, unwrinkled skin. Eat them raw in a salad, lightly steamed or add them at the lasy minute to a stir fry.

Sprouts should be plump and full of moisture; the best ones to try are alfalfa, broccoli or a mild mix of beans and seeds. If you have never tried sprouts before you may like to start with the long bamboo sprouts you often find in Chinese food. Always eat them raw.

Salad leaves are great to add as a side dish to any main course. Choose leaves that are dark green and juicy. Wash well and dress lightly.

PROTEINS We need protein to make new tissue, to grow, and to maintain and repair our tissues. Although this sounds really important, and it is, we only need small amounts of protein. Excess protein is converted into glucose and toxins by the liver so it is good to consider this when you think about your portions. Your plate should be 2/3 vegetables or salad and 1/3 protein. Learn to love vegetable proteins such as legumes (beans,lentils, chick peas etc.) grains (buckwheat, millet,quinoa) seeds, nuts, green leafy vegetables and sprouted seeds. (broccoi, alfalfa) Include a small amount of protein at one or more of your daily meals. Small portions are no bigger than the palm of your hand (not including your fingers).

Vegetable proteins contain a lot of fibre and are good sources of protein and their fat content is practically nothing. Lentils are a really cheap way of getting vegetable protein and fibre in one hit. They look pretty boring but they taste great and if you remember to soak a handful overnight, you just need to change the water and boil them for a few minutes. They are a delicious addition to your veggie stir-fry. The green and brown ones are the tastiest but the small orange ones cook really fast!

Beans should be soaked and try to change the soaking water 2 times before cooking in new water with a bay leaf. This helps to eliminate the gases that can cause flatulence. (gas) Try to soak your beans, lentils and chic peas overnight. All these things can be easily found in corner supermarkets or health food stores in the dried food section. You don't need to know their names in foreign countries, as you will see them in their packets.

Other recommended sources of protein are salmon and tuna. Buy the cans with water, not vegetable oil. Tuna and salmon contain the good fats necessary for healthy skin & hair and will help you stay trim and feeling satisfied. Even better is fresh fish from the market cooked at home. Look for wild Alaskan salmon and grill or poach until just done, let stand for 5minutes.

Chicken should only be organic or free range as added hormones and antibiotics can affect you adversely over the long term. Eggs should also always be organic and try not to eat more than 3 a week.

FATS The best fats to have are nuts, avocados and fantastic seeds. Always have them on hand for emergency hunger pangs when something you shouldn't be eating is tempting you. Pumpkin, sunflower and sesame are the best.

It is continually being documented how dangerous to your health the wrong fats can be so in an effort to make it really simple, here are two of the most nutritious fats around: Olive oil and avocadoes. Use organic extra virgin olive oil on your salads and a teaspoon to cook in. Other fats should come from seeds, nuts and avocadoes. Avoid all other saturated fats such as beef, pork, lamb, un-skinned chicken, duck, whole milk and products made from whole milk such as butter, cream and cheese. Also avoid processed foods with coconut and palm oils. It is also firmly suggested eliminating all margarines and any "food" containing solid vegetable shortening or partially hydrogenated oil or fat of any kind.

WATER The single most important thing you can do for beautiful skin and the health of your body is to drink 2 litres of pure, still water daily. This does not mean expensive bottled water necessarily, but filtered water that is pure. The more water you drink, the less toxins and waste products remain in your system, as they are flushed out by the constant flow of water through your body. The less toxins and waste in the body the easier it is for the body to run efficiently, and get on with the business of keeping your skin clear, hair shiny and your tongue pink. If your tongue is white and coated have one or two days of raw food only, and step up your water intake, but not more than 3 litres until it returns to being pink.

When the body doesn't get enough pure fluids it is unable to eliminate the water soluble toxins and must hold water in the tissues in an attempt to remain hydrated, therefore you may be retaining fluid and feeling bloated because you have not drunk enough water throughout the day, strange as it may seem.

If you have heard this all before it is because it is a well known fact that drinking plenty of water is the true way to beauty, so carry a 500ml bottle with you in your bag and every time you remember, reach into your bag and take a sip. You will find ways to refill your bottle or buy a new one along the course of your day

Avoid drinking a lot of water at meal times and directly after eating as this can dilute the digestive juices, weakening the digestive system.

Have a goal to have drunk 1 litre by noon if you reach the end of the day and realize you haven't drunk enough. Cut it up into a glass every hour, as long as you get your 2 litres daily. Don't wait for the dehydrated headache or the foggy thinking, to tell you to drink more water.

It is important to drink your water throughout the day, not drinking 1 litre before going to bed, otherwise you will be up and down all night to the toilet.

EVERYDAY DIET

The everyday diet is intended as a crash course to the rest of your life. Without studying, measuring or counting, learn to judge your portions and vary your diet so you get the maximum taste enjoyment and fuel that your body needs 6 days a week. On the 7th day you can throw caution to the wind and have what you like, as long as you know you are quite capable of going back to your routine on day 1 again.

Always have breakfast, for the simple reason it will help you control your eating for the rest of the day. Eliminate coffee and sodas completely. This may seem like a hard one but after a while you won't miss it. These drinks contain sugars and stimulants that trigger the body's' natural hormonal responses to stress that cause your body to gain weight around your mid section, so by avoiding them now you will have an easier time controlling your mid section in the long run. Start today!

Forget about having pastries and bread unless it is rye bread or a type of bread with a low glycemic index. Lists of glycemic index quantities are readily available if you feel you need one to check on when it comes to your favourite foods. (www.glycemicindex.com)

Everyday you should have 5 servings of fruit and affordable vegetables, preferably raw. Although you may imagine this is quite hard it is actually easy and affordable. Most importantly, they are beneficial to the health of your skin, nails, hair and digestive system.

As everyone is different, try to find a routine that is most convenient for you to stick to. If you are a late riser and are always rushing around in the mornings, try a breakfast of 3 fruits or a fruit smoothie that you can put in a jar or container to take with you. (Make sure the lid is secure and will not leak the contents into your bag!!) Take an apple and a small handful of nuts with you for mid morning in-case you get hungry especially if can see yourself being tempted by something you shouldn't be eating in the studio. (Open your hand flat and fill only the centre section with nuts and seeds)

Often lunch on a job can be quite late in the day if there are a lot of outfits to do, so always keep a small plastic bag of a few nuts and seeds and a piece of fruit with you. This will give you the energy you need to resist temptation, and help you stay concentrated.

If you have more time in the morning and always have a large appetite try chopping an apple, a banana and 3 or 4 strawberries topped with 3 tablespoons of natural yoghurt and sprinkled with sesame seeds, sunflower seeds and pumpkin seeds. This is an excellent start to the day. The good quality fats in the seeds will keep you satisfied for hours and you will burn off the energy throughout the day.

If you prefer a hot breakfast in the winter, try 3 tablespoons of oatmeal porridge with yoghurt or unsweetened Soya milk. Alternatively 1 egg and the white of a second egg scrambled with parsley and a piece of rye toast or oat cracker. Keep your portions to about the size of your open palm, unless you are eating only fruit. You may have as much fruit as you like in the mornings as you will burn off the natural sugars easily through the day and they supply a lot of fibre and nutrients.

Lunch on a job is often ordered in, but don't despair, there is nearly always something on the menu that will fit into your eating schedule. Try to have salad and a small serving of lean meat a bit smaller than the palm of one hand. Avoid dressings unless they are just olive oil and a small amount of balsamic vinegar. Most dressings contain sugar (including balsamic vinegar) and can have bad fats so ask for Italian dressing or better still, the dressing on the side so you can check it out first. If you are ordering vegetables don't take the ones covered in cheese. Ask if the restaurant is able to make you up a dish of vegetables or choose something on the menu that is as close as possible and ask them to make it without cheese or whatever it is you see doesn't fit. Just make the best out of your situation and if all else fails, eat only a small serving.

If you know you have ordered something that is not so healthy for you, drink 3 glasses of water before it arrives in the studio so you already feel a little fuller. Don't drink any more water once the food arrives, until an hour after you have eaten. Then drink more water than your normal 1 glass every hour. If it was a good choice, keep some of your leftovers for your afternoon snack unless you have something with you from home.

Try to always make lunch something raw, whether it is salad or vegetables. Keeping your lunch raw will make you feel satisfied and full of energy right into the late afternoon. Eat all the salad you want. You need to be moving to help raw food digest so having it late in the day is not the optimum time to eat such a large serving of raw food.

If you are able to make your own choices or are home for lunch you should ideally try to eat a big mixed raw salad. Besides a little lettuce include raw baby spinach leaves (you will never taste them in there if you normally don't like cooked spinach!) cucumber, half a tomato, chopped bell peppers (about 1/4 of a pepper red, orange or green) Add half an avocado and a few sprouts spread over the top and chop a handful of parsley and coriander to sprinkle over the top. If you think it sounds a bit boring, chop in a boiled egg or sheep cheese or some tuna. Your dressing should be 2 or 3 tablespoons of olive oil and a small capful of apple cider vinegar, or the juice of 1/2 lemon, which will be enough just to moisten the salad and not drench it.

Your mid afternoon snack can come around 2 & 1/2 hours after your lunch if you`re a bit hungry. Try a boiled egg or an oat cracker with salmon and a cup of herb tea. Chop up the boiled egg and mix a teaspoon of yoghurt with it, add some ground black pepper and celery salt from the health food store and put it on the oat cracker. Drink a cup of herb tea.

You may also have pieces of bell pepper with hummus or other raw vegetables with a dip made of tuna and yoghurt. Alfalfa sprouts are really healthy and can be mixed with cottage cheese on top of rounds of cucumber for a great healthy snack, have 3 or 4, as there are no starchy carbohydrates!

Having this afternoon snack is very important, as it will stop you from overeating or eating the wrong thing if you are too hungry later.

Dinner should be an important meal as here you are trying to eat the least amount of high-energy food as possible. No starchy carbohydrates should be eaten and only small amounts of lean protein such as organic chicken breast or tuna or salmon.

If you had meat at lunch you can skip the protein at this meal if you like, or include brown rice instead. 60 grams of chicken breast would be enough. (A piece about as big as the palm of your hand) Try to stick to vegetable soup, (made with plenty of celery, and add spinach) a vegetable stir-fry or a big plate of steamed vegetables and brown rice. For example, put one tablespoon of olive oil in a deep frying pan. Add a small chopped leek and lightly fry it until it is wilted, add a handful of broccoli florets and chopped stalk from the broccoli, add about 1/4 cup of filtered water and a teaspoon of organic powdered chicken stock and stir. As the broccoli starts to turn bright green add 1/2 zucchini chopped lengthwise once and sliced in 1cm sections, add it to the leek and broccoli. Cover the pan with the lid for a minute or two while you clean a small handful of button mushrooms and a handful of chopped parsley to finish.

If they are small leave them whole or chop them in half, add them to the vegetables, and cook and stir until nearly all the water is cooked away. This is a delicious stir fry that can be made in minutes and will satisfy you and a friend, or save the leftovers for a mid afternoon snack tomorrow. Serve with a helping of boiled brown rice.

If you have a sweet tooth and are having trouble with cutting the sugar out of your life, try a cup of chai tea with unsweetened soymilk before bed. The liquorice will help to sooth your cravings.

If you are having problems with gas be assured it will pass within the next week, as the routine of plenty of raw food and vegetables will be sorting out a few digestive problems you may have previously had. In the meantime drink fennel tea as this will help. Sip it slowly to get the best results.

If fluid retention is your concern, be sure you are drinking 2-3 litres of water throughout the day, and drink thistle or parsley tea to help eliminate the excess water. Finely chop up a few sprigs of parsley, add hot water, allow steeping for 10 minutes, strain and drink or let it cool and put it in the refrigerator for a cup of cool parsley tea.

Peppermint tea can help if you have a weak digestive system. Sip it slowly.

If you have problems sleeping try a cup of warm unsweetened soymilk.

As far as coffee is concerned, there is growing evidence coffee contributes to elevated cortisol levels which in turn contribute to fat retention especially in the mid section-weight that is the hardest to lose.

IN REVIEW

BREAKFAST
High-energy food such as fruits or eggs with a low glycemic index carbohydrate such as rye toast or oat cracker or oat porridge with unsweetened soymilk or oat porridge with natural unsweetened yoghurt and seeds such as pumpkin, sesame and sunflower.

MID MORNING SNACK
Fruit such as an apple with 6 nuts like almonds, cashews or walnuts or 3 tablespoons of seeds such as pumpkin, sesame and sunflower with a piece of fruit
Note: if you have not had fruit for breakfast eat at least 2 pieces for your mid morning snack. All melons should be eaten alone, as they will move through the stomach faster alone.

LUNCH
Large serving of raw food, such as salad or raw vegetables. If desired a small serving of lean protein such as egg, fish or organic chicken. A protein serving should be no bigger than the middle section of the flat of your hand.
Alternatively you can save your protein serving for dinner and just have a serving of brown rice with your salad.

MID AFTERNOON SNACK
Small serving of protein and low glycemic index carbohydrate. All complex carbohydrates such as raw vegetables are fine, with a lean animal protein or vegetable protein. Cottage cheese on cucumber with alfalfa sprouts. Remember it is a snack, so keep the serving small. (About 5 bites.) If you prefer to drink your snack, try unsweetened soymilk.

DINNER
This should be the lowest energy food of the day as you are finished with your activities and by the time this food is digested you will not be

expending any energy so eat only vegetables in the form of vegetable soup, stir fry vegetables or steamed vegetables and a small serve of protein if you didn't have it for lunch. Eat until you are satisfied

BEFORE BED
A cup of chai tea with unsweetened soymilk or a cup of the above mentioned herbal teas are the best things to have before bed.

NOTES Many people have problems when they initially start drinking more water than they are normally used to. They feel like they are either drinking water or are in the toilet all day. This phase does pass and you will find you are visiting the toilet less frequently as your body adjusts to the new level of hydration. I understand for some jobs on location, it can be difficult to find a toilet but do your best not to get out of your routine, as staying well hydrated is crucial to your skin and weight control.

FOODS TO AVOID This list is mainly made up of foods that basically turn straight to sugar once they hit the stomach. These foods rank high or relatively high on the glycemic index table or are toxic to your liver and although I cannot twist your arm behind your back, if you have the information you will be able to make intelligent choices. Some of these foods will be obvious and others may surprise you, so keep a count of how often you come across these foods and when you collect up in your mind how many of these foods you have eaten then you will be able to judge for yourself whether you are entitled to take your 7th day off.

COFFEE
ALCOHOL (yes all alcohol)
BREAD (sorry!)

Starchy Carbohydrates: Potatoes, carrots, white rice, pasta and all corn. (Whole organic pasta is allowed, but keep it to one serve a week and keep your topping low in fat.) Cakes, biscuits, pastries, pancakes, rice cakes, etc

DAIRY
Large quantities of milk and sweetened commercial dairy foods can cause bloating and contain a type of sugar called lactose, which is hard on the digestive system. Yoghurt is permitted on the everyday diet but stick to the unflavoured, plain yoghurt, mix it with fresh blueberries, strawberries or other fruits in season. Cottage cheese is also allowed due to the high amino acid and protein content.

SWEETS AND SUGAR SUBSTITUTES
Obviously sugar foods should be avoided, but artificial sweeteners are unnatural and will continue to play into your sweet cravings so by eliminating them you will learn to enjoy your foods without cravings. There is also some evidence that sugar substitutes may influence the fat storage hormones in the same way as the real thing!

FATS
The fats you should try to avoid are red meat, pork, bacon, peanut butter and the fats in margarines and processed foods. These particular fats are hard on digestion or are contained in foods that don't supply high nutritional value in comparison to their fat content

SODAS (FIZZY DRINKS)
All sodas should be avoided, including the diet kind for reasons mentioned above.

JUNK FOODS
You know these foods. They are all processed foods such as chips, corn chips, chocolates etc. They contain tons of empty calories and are just not worth it when you count up how much energy it takes to work them off!! Enjoy a small portion if you must on day 7.

FOODS TO INCLUDE

Using some foods to supplement your diet will add to your overall health and the strength of your immune system. They do not need to be added everyday but here is the information for you. I am sure after reading this you will WANT to include them in your diet everyday!!

FLAXSEED OIL

This oil contains the essential fatty acids that the body needs from our diet. These fatty acids may help the body to prevent body fat storage, increase metabolic rate and fat burning, decrease water retention, inhibit mood swings and feelings of depression and if consumed as the flaxseeds themselves, is a high source of fibre. It has one of the highest concentrations commercially available of nutrients that directly support the immune system. Crush linseeds first to release their goodness and sprinkle them on your breakfast or salad. Use the oil only in salads as it should not be heated and buy small quantities and store in the refrigerator as it can have a short lifespan. This goes for the seeds as well if they are crushed. If the taste of the oil is a problem, rub a raw garlic clove over a slice of toast until it is almost gone, distrbute a tablespoon of the oil over the toast and top with slices of tomato and alfalfa sprouts. Can't get healthier than that!

OLIVE OIL

One of the most beneficial oils for the skin and immune system.

LEMONS

Fresh lemon juice is not only an outstanding source of vitamin C, potassium and vitamin B1 but the citric acid in lemons can really stir up the inactive toxic settlements in the body. It can be helpful in controlling hair loss, nervous disorders and skin eruptions. It is a wonderful germicide especially for the certain germ life that exists in influenza and actually encourages the skin to eliminate, which is it's main function. Squeeze the juice of a lemon into your water bottle for it's benefits everyday or substitute the

apple cider vinegar in your salad dressing for lemon juice. Don't expose the juice to the oxygen for too long, as you will loose the valuable potency of the vitamin C.

MUSHROOMS

Some people just hate mushrooms and if that is the case then fine, but they are one of the few rich organic sources of germanium, which increases oxygen efficiency, counteracts the effects of pollutants and increases the body's' resistance to disease. They are extremely low in calories and contain good sources of vitamin B, necessary for your nerves and stress.

PARSLEY

As common as parsley is, it is hard to believe it has such powerful blood purifying qualities and is good for stimulating the bowel. It is good for thought co-ordination and memory. As a tea it has a diuretic effect and can be used to stimulate the kidneys.

APPLES

You know, an apple a day...because apples contain 50% more vitamin A than oranges, necessary for vitality and feelings of well being as well as eye sight, eye infections, glandular balance, acne and rough dry skin. It also helps to ward off colds and other infections. They have more vitamin G (B2) than almost any other fruit, rich in C and also have some vitamin B. These are necessary for digestion, growth, keeping the bones and teeth sound, purifying the blood and are of benefit to the lymphatic system. They sooth and stimulate healthy bowel movements and are beneficial to cleaning the system and in reducing diets. Feel better about apples now?

SPINACH

Popeye's' source of power, this harmless looking leaf may be able to live up to the legend. Only buy dark green fresh leaves and use immediately for the best nutritious value. A fantastic source of vitamins needed for healthy nails, skin, teeth and hair. Spinach is good for the lymphatic, urinary and digestive systems and promotes feelings of vitality and ambition as it plays a significant role in energy production for the body. Its strongly alkaline effect on the body makes tissues elastic and muscles supple, creates grace and a good disposition. Need anymore convincing? (see budget food pg.58) When you notice strong nails and shiny hair it will be totally worth it.

HAPPY FOOD   There are some foods that have a tendency to promote good moods and feelings of comfort and contentedness. We all know this from chocolate and high carbohydrate food like pasta and potatoes. There are many different reasons why some foods make us feel good, but speaking in general terms feelings of low mood and motivation can be improved by avoiding the following;

Blood sugar imbalances, often made worse by stimulants like sugar and caffeine. This doesn't mean if you have a sugar in your coffee you will be depressed. It means that if you are having mood swings, feelings of low motivation or energy and want to help raise your mood and energy, eat foods that will stabilise your blood sugar.

Deficiencies in some B group vitamins, folates, zinc and magnesium as well as fatty acids can further aggrivate depression and low motivation. Vitamins such as B3, B12 (iron) B6 are all key vitamins to help produce the happy chemicals in the brain. Studies of people with clinical depression showed they had low levels of folic acid and EFA (essential fatty acid) and improved when they were given the nutrients.

Chemical imbalances can cause low motivation and/or feeling miserable. Serotonin deficiency can cause the low mood and adrenalin/ noradrenaline can cause low motivation.

Body chemistry is obviously a complicated subject and these are just a few reasons why you may be feeling blue but the essential thing to remember is, if you follow a balanced diet including many or all of the foods listed below

cutting out sugars, stimlants such as caffeine and including whole foods, you will notice a difference in your ability to think clearly, feel full of energy and after a week or two you will even notice your dark circles under your eyes dissapear. Foods can be powerful!

If you are feeling depressed and a week or more on these happy foods does NOT seem to lift your moods you may have an imbalance in your body due to hormones or some other condition. You should visit your doctor or nutritionist to ask him/her to give you a check up based on your feelings as it is sometimes quite easy to treat depression without drugs. It could be as easy as a deficiency in zinc /magnesium or Seratone 5HTP which is readily available at your health food store (100- 300mg daily) which is easily determined by a hair analysis test. It is best to have a Nutritionist look at your total health so you can figure out exactly what the problem is and start a routine, tailor made for you. (to find a nutritionist in London visit www.patrickholford. com)

Food is one essential part of the puzzle to feeling good, activity is another. Exercise is crucial to feelings of well being. Be sure to read the chapter on exercise and get 30 minutes at least of walking every day and 60 min cardio a week. (breaking a light sweat)

Exercise where there is fresh air circulating or grass and trees growing. Don't jog along busy roads or eat fruit and vegetables sold on busy main roads due to the heavy metal pollutants. Of course you should always wash your fruit and vegetables.

THE FOODS Oatmeal, blueberries, strawberries, walnuts, sesame seeds, sunflower seeds, pumpkin seeds, almonds, figs, salmon, herring, mackerel, tuna, sardines, beans, lentils, brown rice, broccoli or alfalfa sprouts (luzerne in German) apples, pears, figs, tomatoes, parsley, spinach, flaxseeds (leinsamen), bellpeppers, broccoli, watercress, green beans, sweet potato and mixed salad leaves

BUDGET

Fortunately for us all, nearly all the food that we need for a healthy existence

can be considered relatively cheap and readily available. Some foods, however, stand out from the crowd as amazingly cheap and nutritious! Before you discount them as boring or not very tasty, try them prepared in the suggested way and you may just be very surprised. In as few as a couple of days you will notice how clear headed and full of energy you feel. Other benefits will be an elevated mood, increased immunity to common colds, regular bowel movements and clear skin. That sounds like just the ticket!

LENTILS High in protein and soluable fibre (more efficient, complete protein than red meat with out the fat) these small and very cheap legumes are a powerhouse of nutrients for the money conscience. High in iron, B vitamins and folate, protecting you against cancer, heart disease and the aging process in general. Soak them overnight, drain and cook in fresh salted water until they are soft but not mushy or broken up. As you would cook pasta al dente, they should be still firm and have a nutty taste.

MUNG BEANS These little green beans are more commonly used as bean sprouts in asian food but they are also a fantastic source of vegetable protein and fibre.(14 gms of protein per cooked cup) They are far less gas producing than other beans and have incredible health benefits from cleansing the blood, by introducing more oxygen (for great skin) to detoxing the liver.

Soak them overnight, as you did with the lentils and boil them in fresh salted water until they are al dente.

OATMEAL Incredibly cheap, filling AND nutritious. High in soluable fibre, vitamin E, selenium, zinc and copper all great for the skin, but also contain minerals good for the nervous system and have proven protection against heart disease and some cancers. Having a positive impact on controlling blood sugar levels and having antioxident qualities that kill free radicals, it seems it can also keep you looking good! Advocated by weight loss gurus because of its low fat content
Put 1 part oatmeal to 2 parts liquid (soy milk/water) and bring to the boil. Take off the heat and let stand until cool enough to eat. For extra through the roof health, add crushed flaxseeds. There is no healthier start to the day for sustained energy and health properties.

BROCCOLI Being one of the most powerful vegetable weapons against cancer and tumors should be enough to include it in your diet everyday, but the fact that it is cheap and versatile is such a delicious bonus. Even better is broccoli seed sprouts. These cheap and tasty sprouts can provide 10 – 100 times the power of broccoli to neutralize cancers. Broccoli contains Vit C, folate, calcium, Vit E and coenzyme Q10. All these protect your eyes, heart, skin, bones

FOOD

and immune system. Eat it raw, lightly steamed, made into soup or in a stir fry. Always buy crisp (no floppy stem) dark green tightly packed small heads. If the leaves are still on the stem, look to see if they are wilted to check the freshness.

SPINACH Ok, no one is making a meal out of spinach alone but it is cheap and just maybe one of the worlds superfoods. The list of its nutrients seems endless, chlorophyll for oxygenating and cleaning the blood, coenzyme Q10 for heart heath and skin, Vit B,C,E and Omega 3 fatty acid. It plays a significant role in energy production for the body, defending our skin against damage from the sun, eye sight health, defending the body against heart disease, a long list of cancers from lung, skin, oral, stomach, to breast and colon cancer. Drop a few washed leaves into your stir fry at the last minute or pop a handful amongst the salad leaves, you will never taste the difference. Have it just wilted as a side dish to salmon or in mashed potatoes.

CANNED TOMATOES Are a great way to make a pasta sauce, a ragout or a chilli con carne. As the base to a vegetable bonanza or simply cooked and reduced with Thyme and a handful of mushrooms. Add a tablespoon of tomato paste to taste and some chilli and kidney beans for a healthy cheap meal, available everywhere for a cheap and easy meal base.

PASTA Using spelt or wholemeal pasta is preferable to white pasta, only because it will affect the blood sugar in a more sustained, positive way. Pasta is definitely cheap and filling but when it comes to nutrition everything depends on what you put on it! Vegetable Bolognese made with your own choice of vegetables and a can of peeled tomatoes is probably the best way to go as anything creamy will negatively affect your waistline. A cheap, easy way with pasta, if you like garlic and chilli, is to gently fry chopped garlic and fresh chilli (remove the seeds if you don't like it burning hot and wash your hands well with soap and water IMMEDIATELY after chopping it!!) in a couple of tablespoons of olive oil. Don't brown the garlic and it is ready when the chilli is soft (about 2-3 minutes) Toss the cooked pasta in the oil/garlic/chilli mix and top with grated parmesan or another favorite hard cheese and finely chopped parsley. Done!

APPLES Satisfying and nutritious, apples will have a positive effect on your waistline, skin and digestion, are cheap and easily accessible. The best thing to take with you for a snack on the run and with a handful of nuts or seeds, will keep you satisfied for a couple of hours. As dessert they satisfy the sweet craving and the crunch squashes any stimulant craving you may have. All round a great staple in your diet. Try to have 2 or 3 every day!

LINGERIE DIET

There is always a job coming up or a special occasion when you just have to drop a little bit of weight to look your optimal best.

Obviously someone who needs to loose more than just a little bit should take their time and do it slowly by following the everyday diet and increasing their exercise.

As a model you will be doing more than the minimum 30 minutes daily of sustained light exercise but for those intending to do the lingerie diet it is important for you to realize this is not a diet that should be continued for longer than the one or two week period it is intended for. Your nutrient requirements for nails, skin, hair and other bodily functions are more important than compromising them for lack of motivation to exercise more.

Remember, this is not a long-term diet and considering your bodily beauty, as a whole, is far more valuable to your clients and your physical and mental well being than being thin.

The thing to consider about this diet is, your absolute commitment to it for it to effectively work. Alcohol, tea, coffee, sodas, dairy, fruit, bread, pasta, rice, carrots and starchy foods are strictly forbidden. Drinking a lot of water throughout the day is absolutely essential for the diet to work, otherwise you will become constipated and will feel and be even fatter! Exercise is necessary every day, even if you are doing only 30 minutes fast walking.

If you are expecting great results weight train either arms and abs one day and legs, butt and back the next, but lift light weights in addition to your 30 min cardio. Even if you are only lifting two 1-litre bottles of water, keep up high repetitions of 3 sets of 20 or 4 sets of 15 if you are not already training.

THE DEAL

The basic plan of this diet is to eat small portions often, of protein and slow burning carbohydrate, to rev up the metabolism and keep the body burning energy steadily throughout the day. No sugars or high fat content foods are eaten, as you are trying to reduce your high-energy intake, so that is why no dairy or fruit (or chocolate!!) as it contains sugars. The protein takes a lot of energy to digest and assimilate, so include it at every meal. It also feeds your muscles and vegetable proteins will be more efficient as they have their own enzymes and minimal fat. Try to eat a mouthful of protein first. The last meal of the day is just protein and vegetables. Try to have vegetable protein at dinner, as this will also reduce the fat content. You should notice the reduction start in about day 3. Most importantly, is to drink all the assigned water throughout the day. Without drinking the water you may put on weight and will have less energy. The trick is to always have something stoking your metabolism but not taxing the digestive process too hard either. No starchy carbohydrates either as they don't mix well with proteins and supply too much energy.

Don't constantly weigh yourself it will make you anxious and preoccupied with your weight, try to stay busy doing chores and castings for the first 3 days, just to keep yourself occupied, although it is best to do this diet when you are not working. After 3 days you should see the first real results and will be over the hump of getting your body used to a new routine. It will also keep you motivated, as the results are always inspiring.

If you are at work, bring along 3 snacks as you may not be able to break for lunch when your plan says it is time to eat, if that is the case, just eat less at lunch. Use one for your mid morning snack, one for lunch (if it isn't coming when you need to eat) and the last one for your mid afternoon snack which should be 2 and 1/2 hours after you ate lunch. Remember, you are just stoking the fire every few hours. (An ideal lunch is chicken or turkey breast with a small salad with either no dressing, or the juice of 1/2 lemon.)

Set the alarm on your phone to a special ring every 2 and half-hours, unless you are at work. That will remind you it is time to eat. Don't take this tip for granted. It is really easy to get carried away and forget to eat so regularly. Here is now, one last tip that will guarantee this diet will be a great success; don't cheat! Drink all your water plus clear vegetable soup with your snacks to increase your water consumption and to make you feel fuller. You can bring your soup to work in an empty jar with a tight and secure lid, but don't forget to drink the assigned amount of water as well as the soup.

THE DIET

When you get up have a glass of warm water and the juice of 1/2 lemon. Change into your sport clothes and exercise. Shower and eat breakfast within 30 minutes of exercising. You may choose to shower after breakfast.

BREAKFAST   Start your metabolic engine for the day with one of the following:
Scrambled egg and an oat cracker or
Hummus spread on an oat cracker or
Avocado spread on a rye crisp bread sprinkled with pumpkin/sesame/sunflower seeds topped with sprouts (alfalfa or broccoli) or
4 strips of cooked chicken breast wrapped inside a lettuce leaf
Have also a cup of herbal tea or a glass of sugar free organic Soya milk
In the following 2 hours, drink at least 350ml water each hour. In one glass of water mix in 2 teaspoons of psyllium husks and drink immediately. Follow with another drink either of water or herbal tea.

MID MORNING SNACK   Have clear vegetable soup with your snack each time even if you feel satisfied by the snack alone. Try canned salmon on an oat cracker, or a boiled egg, mashed with a small teaspoon yoghurt (no servings of yoghurt are allowed but a teaspoon of natural yoghurt is ok) salt and pepper to taste. Hummus is delicious on an oat cracker or a tablespoon of steamed spinach from leftovers the night before, with 2 or 3 small strips of cooked chicken or salmon. Or 10 mixed walnuts, cashews and almonds if you are in the city or on the run. Just keep your snacks to no more than a few mouthfuls to have with your soup. Remember you will be eating again soon anyway. You can add unlimited sprouts to any of your snack choices (alfalfa or broccoli or mixed)

INBETWEEN   Drink at least 350 ml water each hour for the next 2 hours add the juice of 1/2 lemon to each glass

LUNCH   Lunch should consist or 60g of good quality protein (about the size of your palm) such as organic chicken breast without the skin, skinless turkey breast, wild salmon fillet or tuna (fresh or from the can) a small side salad or steamed veggies that will fit in both your hands. Dressing can be olive oil and lemon juice.

IN BETWEEN   Drink 350ml water each hour for the following 3 hours. In one glass mix 2 teaspoons of psyllium husks and drink immediately.

MID AFTERNOON SNACK (SEE MID MORNING)

Drink 350ml water each hour for the next 2 hours. Add the juice of 1/2 lemon to each glass.

DINNER   Dinner is basically the same as lunch, but go for some variety so you don't get bored. You can make a vegetable soup (no carrots or potatoes) and add 2 tablespoons of cooked chic peas or lentils to your bowl. Alternatively try a stir-fry of leek, broccoli, zucchini, mushroom, lentils and mung beans. The recipe is called The Bomb Stir Fry in FAVORITE RECIPES Pg.118

NOTE   Don't miss out your snacks as they are essential to keep the metabolism burning and they will control your hunger.
Try to eat dinner early and go to bed in no less than 2 hours after you have eaten. Drink 2 cups of parsley / thistle tea if you feel hungry or antsy. These teas are great for getting rid of the excess fluid and will help you feel lighter. Other herbal teas are also fine if you prefer peppermint for digestion or camomile to help you relax. You should aim to be in bed by 10:30pm. This is an important part of resting and repairing from your exercise. (It also allows your digestive system to get into the correct rhythm.)

This is not an easy diet to stick to and is only intended for a quick burst to cut you into shape for a body job such as lingerie or swimwear. For a more sustained weight loss program the everyday diet is ideal as it has satisfying and healthy foods that will gently help your body to find its shape. The things that will hinder your weight loss more than any other factors are: not drinking enough water, eating high salt and bad fat foods and consuming too many empty calories so think carefully about chocolate, chips, sodas (including diet sodas) and sugars!

TRIP DIETS

Generally speaking by the time you are on a trip it is a bit late for diets and you really should just relax and enjoy your job, the team and your environment. Photographic trips can take you to some of the most beautiful locations in the world without anything for you to arrange, so enjoy the time and give your team all your love and help you can, so everyone can enjoy the experience. There is nothing worse than a model insisting on special food requirements when in a foreign country. This can really irritate the rest of the team, spoil what is a fabulous cultural experience for everyone and make you seem obsessive.

If you do have a special job coming up and still need to drop a couple of kilos stay on the ball by avoiding all alcohol. Drink plenty of bottled, still water, which will be available for the rest of the team as well. Eat plenty of fruit in the first half of the day, if you are a bit worried you are not getting enough water. Avoid fruit at the end of the day as the sugars will make you puffy and bloated the next morning. Keep as much raw food, such as salads, in your diet as possible and grab a couple of boiled eggs from the breakfast buffet for your afternoon snacks. At dinner avoid bread and stick to steamed fish and ask if you can replace potatoes with extra veggies.
Places like Morocco will often have exotic grains and foods prepared in exotic combinations so just make your portions small if you are unsure and enjoy the new experiences while making up for it the next day if you feel you may have overindulged.

DO I HAVE A PROBLEM?

If you find yourself constantly thinking about food or obsessing over it, it really is up to you to try to find your perspective on the subject.

There is a lot of evidence emerging that suggests that stress itself can be responsible for mobilising hormones such as cortisol that are responsible for causing weight gain especially around your midsection. For this very reason your stressing and obsessing over your food can be the one thing that is making you feel fat and frustrated by your inability to lose the weight you want to. Restrict your diet to ONLY whole foods if you have stubborn fat around your butt or thighs. This fat is exacerbated by toxins.

Have you ever noticed the times you managed to lose weight without even thinking about it was when you were freshly in love or busy with friends on holidays or just busy enjoying yourself? So, make a deal with yourself to avoid the things you know are blatantly fattening like ice-cream, candy and potato chips and start including whole foods like apples, strawberries, broccoli and mushrooms and drinking plenty of water and forgetting about weighing yourself and wishing for a thinner body.

In one month of this "mental holiday" weigh yourself again and you will realize the mental anguish you put yourself through on a daily basis is just not worth it. When that little voice pops up in your head that says " you are too fat" or "she has the body I want!" consciously stop and say to that voice "NO! I am on holiday from your criticisms and I will enjoy a month free of that kind of thinking!", and go about your day. Even if that voice pops up 20 times a day, each time dismiss it, as you are on holidays from the negative talk!

EMERGENCY HEALTH

There is nothing worse than being sick away from home. If you are on a trip, your team will be there to help you with anything serious, so don't hesitate to call the makeup artist or stylist to tell them if you have a fever or need something from a doctor. Waiting until it is really serious or in the middle of the night is inconsiderate and can be really stressful for the others so always talk to someone you trust in the team early on, if you suspect it could be something serious. It can happen to anyone so don't feel like you are a burden.

There are many remedies you can use from the kitchen for a lot of not so serious things, so don't trouble others in a team for anything that is not serious.

PIMPLES A simple remedy for pimples can be a tiny amount of crushed garlic clove and a squirt of vitamin E oil. Combine these two for a fast acting healer. Only use vitamin E oil at night as it is destroyed by light. The combination of the two really attacks the infection and heals the eruption fast. If it feels like it is burning use less garlic otherwise the spot could turn dark brown.

HEARTBURN This is one that can keep you up all night! Try sipping warm water or a glass of Coca-Cola. If this happens to you often, include some over the counter tablets for heartburn in your dot bag.

CONSTIPATION Use psyllium husks to add extra fibre to your diet or if you have problems with constipation on trips often. Increase water intake, also try a little lemon juice and the yolk of a raw egg in a glass of orange juice as a mild laxative. Daily Magnesium supplements of 400mg will help if it is a long term problem. Try Orthica brands' Magnesium 400. It includes selenium, calcium and zinc

FEVER If you have nothing else for a fever (such as ferrum phosphoricum from the homeopathic chemist.) drink the juice of 1 lemon in hot water. Sip it slowly. If the fever progresses, take 2 aspirin and continue the lemon juice and hot water. A tepid bath can also help to bring the fever down.

COLDS OR FLU Drink the juice of 1 lemon in hot water. Take Vitamin B and C to support your immune system and try to relax or just take a sauna without the sport. If you have a fever, do not have a sauna.

NAUSEA If you suspect you may have eaten something that did not agree with you or is suspicious (seafood, like muscles for example) then it is best to let your nausea follow it's course as the body needs to purge the poison out of your system. Take comfort in the fact that these things never often last for longer than 12 hours and tomorrow you will be fine again. In the mean time, to speed your recovery, drink plenty of water between severe nausea attacks and lie down and keep warm.

SORE THROAT Use apple cider vinegar diluted, to gargle with 3 times a day to improve the condition. Anaesthetic / Antiseptic throat lozenges will numb and treat the throat if you have them with you or can buy them at your location.

SKIN FUNGUS Skin fungus can show up if you have recently spent time at the beach. It looks like white or pale spots on your arms, back and face usually. Before rushing off to the doctor try Selsun Blue anti dandruff medicated shampoo. Use it first on your arms and back in-case it stings. Lather it on the skin and let it stay for 4 or 5 minutes and then rinse it off. If it doesn't irritate the skin use it on your face carefully avoiding the eyes. You may need to use it 2 or 3 times but it is a cheap solution to a common problem that can really be a problem for work.

COMMON DEFICIENCIES

White Marks on the nails is a sign of zinc deficiency. As the absorbtion of zinc is inhibited by wheat, try to cut out wheat prducts for a while, increase foods containing zinc and add a supplement of around 20mg a day. Foods to include are pumpkin and sunflower seeds as well as Oatmeal.

Pimples tend to occur when there is congestion or imbalances. The best thing to do is to tackle both. Increase your illimination through the bowels and bladder by increasing water and fibre in the diet. Go for 2 litres of pure water a day and have plenty of fruit for breakfast, salad for lunch and vegetables and grains for dinner. Add 1-2 teaspoons of psyllium husks to a large glass of water midmorning for extra fibre without the calories.

Splitting, chipping nails can be due a deficiency in zinc (see white marks on nails) and too little essential fatty acids (fish, nuts and seeds) Drink Nettle Tea to help absorb nutrients. Take Silica tissue salts (naturopathic supplement)

Dark Circles under the eyes can be hereditary or due to kidney weakness. Increase your water intake and also include 2-3 glasses of cranberry juice every day. Cut out sugar.

Puffy eyes can be due to water retention, poor sleep, drinking alcohol or poor nutrition. (consuming soy sauce can also result in puffy eyes) Use splashes of cold water or a cold compress for immediate results and drink plenty of fluids including 2-3 cups of Nettle tea. Eat well and get to bed before 10.30pm to see outstanding results.

Cracked corners of the mouth is due to a Vitmin B2 deficiency (riboflavin) Increase your fruit and green leafy vegetables including Parsley. Take a B group Vitamin supplement which includes at least 50mg of Vit B2.

EXERCISE

Keeping your body in form is obviously one of the main criteria for a model.

Running around doing go sees is only part of your fitness regime. Each person will have a different schedule of exercise that will keep them in form but remember, being fit will also give you stamina for the long days in the studio or on location.

You will need to find a routine that will be easy for you to incorporate into a busy and irregular schedule, so find something you are able to do easily everywhere such as jogging and floor exercises, which is what we will be focusing on in this chapter.

If you are unsure about which fitness plan is for you, join a local gym and get a fitness assessment. Some gyms will offer a membership for 2 weeks at a time or for a certain amount of visits. This is ideal as you won't have to pay for the time you are not there, if you travel a lot.

Mention to the trainer that you would like to have a routine that includes floor exercises that you can do anywhere, without weights or machines. Your exercise plan should include aerobic exercise for fitness and stamina, as well as weights for strength and body sculpting. Instead of travelling with weights use two 1.5litre bottles of water and increase the repetitions or / and the number of sets (for example 15 repetitions of lifting a weight is one set and you might do 3 or 4 sets with a 30 second break between sets)

If you have never worked out before it is best to train with an instructor first, so you can fully understand form and isolating the muscle. Form means the way you hold your body and perform the exercise. It is very important to have good form when doing your exercises as this will assure you maximum results and minimum strain or injury. Isolating the muscle in your mind and concentrating on the specific muscle being targeted can increase the effectiveness of your workout. Being precise with your workout can lead to better results.

Before you start your exercise routine take a few minutes to very gently stretch and warm up. Don't take this part of the routine for granted, as it is important to avoid injuring muscles and joints. Standing all day in the studio will be a nightmare if you have a painful knee or ligament injury. Likewise don't overdo it in the beginning. It is a recipe for failure to stick to a workout plan and can be really painful if you are not used to exercise.

AEROBIC

This is the kind of exercise that burns the calories. Remember, if you want to lose weight you have to burn off more than you consume in food. The best way to burn calories is to exercise moderately for an extended period. This means at least for 40 minutes consecutively every other day. You should be breathing heavier, but still comfortably through your nose only and will be heating up just enough to break a slight sweat. By heavier aerobic exercise, like jogging for example, you will be increasing your heart and lung capacity and improving your fitness level as well as increasing the metabolism, which is the speed of which your body burns fuel even when resting. Increasing the metabolism can also help if you have poor circulation and suffer from cold hands and feet.

By lifting light weights but with many repetitions, you will create muscle tone. When you increase the weight you will increase the bulk of the muscle. This in turn will need more energy from the body so will also therefore burn fat around the muscle for fuel.

An ideal fitness routine will include parts from all of these exercises, as you will certainly work on your fitness level when exercising aerobically to lose weight. As the weight is dropped and you find exercising easier you will naturally increase your load gradually. Lifting weight can be addictive so be careful not to become in any way bulky. Models always need to be lean so they will look good even in layered, bulky or tight clothes. High repetitions with low weights are recommended unless you are specifically trying to sculpt a specific area such as the arms or calf muscles.

Some areas are always difficult to spot reduce and becoming obsessed with them is often the first step in becoming overly neurotic. Try to keep your perspective by asking a good friend whose opinion you trust, to tell you honestly if you need to do to lose weight. Then, believe them and let it go or work on it honestly and in a disciplined manner. There is no point in eating junk food and coffee and then complaining about cellulite that just won't budge!!

THE MINIMUM amount of exercise you should aim for is at least 30 minutes of light exercise such as walking daily and 60 minutes of aerobic activity a week. You can break this up into 3 20 minute increments but you must break a sweat.

HOTEL ROOM EXERCISES

If you are away a lot it is easy to get out of your routine so always try to do your hotel room exercises or if the hotel has a gym or pool do some aerobic exercise. As mentioned before, water bottles can be substituted for light weights and take 4 or 5 minutes to warm up by walking on the spot and reaching above your head breathing deeply and stretching very gently. Flexing the feet and bending in the knees will warm up and send the blood to the muscles and joints ready for exercise.

SQUATS One of the most important exercises for your hips, back, knees and general well being, squats can improve your overall athletic ability when done correctly.

Start with the feet about shoulder width apart, toes slightly pointing out. Keep your head up, looking slightly above you. Keeping your stomach or midsection tight with your weight on your heels, slowly descend keeping the head up and squeezing your butt and thighs. Imagine you are sitting down into a chair behind you. As you start sending your butt down, lift your arms up and out infront of you. Focus, to keep the control in your body. Good form is important in all exercises, to avoid injury and improve strength.

Points to remember:
- Keep your weight on your heels
- Don't just sink, control the movement with your hip flexors
- Keep your butt pointed out and down without arching your back
- Knees should stay straight over the line of the feet
- Come up on the same path as you went down
- Don't roll forward or drop your shoulders on your up path
- Stand as tall as you can at the end of the squat, arms above you

Take your time perfecting your squats as they should be the backbone of your routine and will help to improve your power and stamina. Do as many as you can manage to do perfectly and build from there. You will be amazed how much power a few squats can give you and in no time you will have a perky butt, rock solid thighs and knock out posture.

LUNGES While holding a large water bottle in each hand, lunge forward and bend the forward knee at a 90 degree angle before pushing yourself back into the starting position. Keep your back straight and repeat using the other leg. Do at least 2 sets of 10 on each leg. These will get the blood pumping!

SIT UPS Hook your feet under the end of the bed if you can, or put your lower legs on the bed forming a 90 degree angle and sit up just far enough to lift the shoulder blades off the floor. Support the neck with your hands but lift your chin up to the ceiling as you go. It may be easy in the beginning but 3 sets of 10 will get you grunting in the end!

BICEPTS CURLS AND TRICEPT LIFTS Sit on the edge of the bed and alternate a 1.5 litre bottle of water for your bicep curl weight. Three sets of 15 should do the trick. Triceps can be worked by lying on the bed with your head close to the edge but not over it. Lift your arm with the water bottle in your hand over your head so it is over the edge of the bed. Keeping the arm stable, bend the elbow and straighten it above the head. With the free hand touch the underside of your arm to feel the muscle working. 3 sets of 10

FLOOR EXERCISES Lay on the floor, on your side supporting your head with your hand and the elbow on the floor. With your free hand support yourself, with the hand on the floor opposite your stomach. Move both your feet slightly forward so you are not in an exact straight line.

Remembering to use your front arm for support, brace your stomach and lift your top leg off the bottom one about as wide as your hips. Swing it out in front of you and pretend to kick something lightly with two taps. Swing the leg behind you being careful not to roll with your hips backwards and do the kick -kick behind you too. Keeping your torso stable by bracing your stomach muscles, supporting yourself with the hand on the floor, and keeping the movement controlled.Repeat this 10 times.

Do a high kick with your top leg towards your head. Repeat 10 times.

Again with your top leg, draw a big circle with your pointed toes in the air 5 times, then change the direction and do another 5.

Now draw 10 small circles not higher than your hip height with your toes in the air and then 10 in the opposite direction.

Kick your straight leg out at hip height in front of you as far as you can, bend the leg and move the bent leg behind you without arching your back or rolling your hips, keep the control with the hand on the floor and your stomach muscles.

Straighten the leg once it is behind you, bring it back infront of you again to the starting position.

Do this 5 times then the other way around; bring the bent knee up towards the chest and slowly straighten the leg out, sweep it behind you without rolling then bend the knee and bring it forward, a bit like bicycling.

Change sides and repeat. Do these exercises twice on each side every day you are away and watch those saddlebags melt away!!

Take a few minutes to stretch your legs, arms and lower back to help to elongate the muscles and keep you flexible. When you are finished take 2 more minutes (or more) to lie on your back and simply relax, breathe deeply and feel the blood rushing around your body. Take a moment to thank your body for being so beautiful and glorious in its daily function, giving you energy and happiness, carrying you through your wonderful life!

CASTINGS

A "Casting" is an appointment to see a client, casting agent, photographer or Production Company who have a scheduled job and need a model to be booked.

They are usually looking for a specific type or have a strong idea of the kind of character or type they want for the job. If your portfolio doesn't really have the type they are looking for in it, make an effort to dress the part.

Your role is either to fit the type they are looking for, or wow them with your lovely personality.

Try to get as many details as possible from your booker about what they are looking for, who the client is, what the job is for, how long the job is and if it is on location or in the studio.

Do your best to look the part, and imagine yourself as the client. What would he / she be looking for? If you feel like you are not really the type they are looking for, try to BE the type inside, like an actor taking on a different character.

Try not to be over enthusiastic or talk too much, but if they ask you questions, answer with enthusiasm and positivity and use every opportunity to laugh. People LOVE happy people. You will bring a little happiness into their dull day, and if you can manage to pay them an honest compliment, do so. It will make them feel good and remember you.

A go see is an appointment to introduce yourself to a client or photographer. This is a quick, general "get to know you" and a chance for you to make a positive impression. Don't miss this chance to show the client or photographer your personality, as well as your portfolio. Sometimes people can make jobs happen with you in mind if you inspire them!

If you know you have a tendency to be over enthusiastic and easily excitable, stop and take a few deep breaths to compose yourself before you go in. Relax your shoulders, neck and face. Be conscience of speaking in your true voice. Over excitement can raise your tone a bit.

You will sound more confident and composed if you use the tone you speak to yourself with, and not the high pitch you use when greeting your dog. Smile before you speak.

Try to make a mental note of their name so you can use it in conversation and at the end of your meeting. Take their lead in the conversation and laugh out loud whenever you get a good chance to. Don't criticize yourself, your portfolio or anyone else. If they are critical, just smile and say, "really?" Always say thank you when you leave, but don't thank them for their time. They should be happy you came to introduce yourself to them, and in some countries they may think it sounds a bit sarcastic so just say thank you and their name if you remember it. Take your cue from the client if they want to chat, otherwise keep it short, happy and sweet.
ALSO: See FINAL TIPS pg. 116

WHAT TO WEAR

Basically it is up to you what you wear on castings and gosees but if you can dress the part it is always easier for the client to imagine you IN the part. Ever heard the expression "she is perfect"?

Another important part of dressing for gosees is to consider the city you are in and the weather. For example London is a city where people love to have fun with fashion so dressing in a very eclectic way is really acceptable but if you are in Milan dressing in sexy clothes can make you the "meat in the sandwich" for the guys on the street. Paris can be quite liberal but with a high religious population it is best to err on the less sexy side. Hamburg is usually cold anyway and the clients will think you are ridiculous if you are over dressed, so stay low-key in the German cities. They will appreciate a very understated cool, with maybe one stylish piece.

Generally, Europe appreciates the subtleness of your fashion and sexual expression so go more for something cute, sweet or colourful to bring yourself the attention. Jeans are always a good staple and cool is always in fashion. Remember you will be running around the city all day so wear comfortable shoes, which are in fashion anyway, or bring your high ones with you if you have a swimwear or lingerie casting, as they make your legs look long and your body curvy. Keep your „looks" down to a minimum as you will not be able to travel with a lot of luggage.

MAKEUP

Makeup for a full day of castings and gosees can be a disaster if you start off with too much on. It is really important that your skin looks great no matter who you are seeing, so start with a sheer base or a tinted moisturiser that is exactly the colour of your skin. Try Stilas' sheer colour tinted moisturiser or Mac's face and body foundation. (Mix two colours on the back of your hand to get the exact colour for summer and winter)

I am sure that the bronzer you use on a Friday night looks fabulous but if people are going to be looking right into your face in daylight, you should try to look as fresh and makeup free as possible. Use a mirror in the daylight to apply a slightly yellow toned, heavy pigmented concealer (like the one at Mac or Stila) to dark circles and spots or pimples, with a brush. If you have put too much concealer on and they are too light, dab them with the pad of your finger, up and down on the spot until they disappear when you look at your whole face in the mirror. Do the same with any redness around your nose.

You can also try one of the fabulous under eye concealers on the market and pat the concealer into ONLY the dark areas under your eyes. If you are having trouble seeing where the shadows are, make sure the light is evenly on your face first. Dip your chin down and look into the mirror. See the dark shadows, fix your eyes on them, and slowly raise your chin until you are looking straight at yourself as you would to people that you meet. Cover only the grey areas. One great under eye concealer is Guerlain precious light smoothing illuminator. Another is Yves Saint Laurent radiant touch. Apply them as precisely as you can with the applicator brush and then pat the colour to centre it and just blend the outside edges.

If you have white circles when you look straight into the mirror at your whole face, pat the white areas until they fade.

Do not wipe at the area under your eyes. This is also an ineffectual way to soften the excess; you will just be sliding it into the wrong place. If patting with the pad of your finger doesn't immediately lessen the problem, use a Q-tip and step back from the mirror a little so you can see the whole picture better.

Powder is a very underestimated tool of makeup artists. Loose transparent powder applied with a natural haired brush will give you the best results. Powder will not only make your sheer base and foundation stay put longer, it will create a medium for the base, concealer and powder to look invisible.

Don't be tempted to press powder into the face with a powder puff. This will make the makeup look thick and get old quicker.

Use your brush to fix the concealer on pimples by dabbing at them with the brush. Whisk away any excess powder with the brush. Try buying your natural hair brushes at the art store where they are cheaper than at a cosmetic counter.

If your skin gets oily during the day use cigarette rolling papers to press onto the oily parts around your nose mouth and forehead to mop up the oil, then lightly whisk the powder over your face again, with the brush, to freshen it up.

Most girls wouldn't dream of leaving the house without mascara on and curling their lashes but just curling your lashes can also be quite a cool look, team it with just blusher and lip gloss for a really fresh look.

If you must wear mascara but find by the end of the day you look like a racoon, be sure to check on it frequently throughout the day. Use a small hand mirror or a compact for a quick check. If there are black flecks of mascara also falling onto your face it may be time to throw your mascara away and invest in a new one. They normally don't last longer than 6 weeks to a few months and there are many different types on the market from clumpy thick ones with fibres, to fine ones like Maybelline in the pink and green container.

You will get a bit more oomph out of it, if you apply it first in the traditional way, moving the wand slightly back and forth in the lashes so you wiggle it into the roots, and then sliding it up through the lashes. Then, dab at the lashes about in the middle of the hairs and onto the tips. It leaves more mascara on the lashes. Curl the lashes with a heated eyelash curler. The heat comes from a tiny AAA battery and by pressing the lashes into an extreme curl, you will easily curl the lashes without pressing the mascara flat and risking pinching yourself.

NOTE Professional models know how to make life easier for themselves and the makeup artist by looking in the opposite direction of where the wand is when the makeup artist is putting on the mascara. A makeup artist can tell how experienced a girl is by whether she knows this trick or not.

When the makeup artist is putting mascara on the inside corner of the lashes, you look to the outside of your face and down to the floor.

As she moves the wand to the outside part of the lashes move your eye, still looking down, to the inside, so the eye she or he is working on is looking in the other direction. This stretches the eyelash line and makes application easier.

Blusher comes in and out of fashion and if you choose to use it, it should enhance your bone structure, so use richer colours under the bone at the side of your face up onto the high point of the apple of your cheek (you may need to smile at yourself in the mirror to find that point) Brighter colours can be used just on the apple of your cheek but never put the colour up high on the bone close to your eyes unless you are trying to be theatrical or are going to a 70's party. Always blend your blusher well to avoid just having blobs or stripes of colour.

Lip pencils have gone out of fashion to line the lips with. We are glad not to see the weary lip line with the lipstick eaten off anymore.
A sheer glossy lipstick can do wonders to make you look like you are groomed and have made an effort even if you had absolutely no time at all. Always have one that lives in every bag you own, so you are never without it. Pots or wands are great, but watch your application. You don't want to look like you were just feasting on greasy fish and chips!

BEACH SKIN

If you are going to a casting or party and want to have the sun kissed look of J Lo's skin on your body try mixing a dark shade of Macs' face and body foundation with Nivea Silk Shimmer Lotion or Mac Strobe cream. Apply it well and be careful not to get it on your clothes.
It is perfect for legs, arms, shoulders and neck but blend it out before getting to the face or close to your clothes if they are light in skin colour.
It is not suitable to use on your face as you need to have a little more control of the shine on your face otherwise you could end up looking like a butter ball. Makes the skin look fabulous!

If your skin is already dark enough from using a fake tan or you are lucky enough to have naturally dark skin, try Penaten Baby Oil-Gel. Don`t use it to moisturize the skin as it doesn't really penetrate the skin, it is the paraffin that makes the skin feel soft, but it really does pump up the shine factor like you see on girls in the music videos. Great for legs, arms, stomach, back and shoulders but be careful if you have a bony chest as it can really accentuate the bones. Use it only on the high points of your bosom to catch the light and accentuate their fullness.

CASTING TYPES

There are some general types of models that clients often look for. By using your common sense when it comes to presenting yourself and some subtle styling changes, you can give the right impression with very little effort. Some clients will specifically request certain hair coloured models too. Some agents will give the blonde haired castings to brunettes too, just to keep them busy and seeing as many clients as possible. The theory of this is that the client might be so impressed by a girl they will include her in the job or a future job regardless of her hair colour. Unfortunately some clients JUST want to see brunettes or JUST blondes so if they flip through your portfolio in record time or don't want to look at it, don't be too disappointed.

If the client has asked for some specific type or has a special request and you are unsure what your agent means, ask for details so you can give the client the best impression. Here are a few general types.

SPORTY   generally means fresh, young and casual.

SHOW   castings are about several things, your proportions, your "look" and the way you walk. Showing your great legs is always a plus.

WOMANLY / MOTHER　This type is generally for Commercials. Maybe they want you to be with a baby or a small child. Try to keep your look simple and uncomplicated

CHANGING YOUR TYPE ON THE RUN　It can be very often the case that you may have a lot of castings for specific, but very different types in one day. It could go from sporty to motherly and back to a music video. Do your best to look the part by putting your hair into a high pony tail for the sporty casting and leaving it down and taking off any chunky jewelery for the motherly one. You can be creative if you wish, by bringing scarves to tie around your hair or to loop through the loops of your jeans to make you look more sexy or funky. Use your imagination but remember you are going for something that will just make it easier for the client to imagine you in that job. They will want to see your hair and don't overdo your makeup! Hats can give you something to create an entrance with and maybe something to play with if you have to dance around in front of a video camera for a music video, but don't over style yourself to the point of hiding your greatest asset, YOU!

WORKING THE MARKETS

Essentially, markets are different countries, with the variation of work within that market.

Most have a variety of work but are recognized as especially good in one area or another.

When someone talks about different markets and what they are like, it is best to listen intently and suck up as much information from your fellow models and bookers as possible.

The information can be valuable for you to learn from, as different markets offer different things and markets can change, so it is best to always keep your ear to the ground. Each of these markets have specific clients that dominate and therefore this will constitute the bulk of the jobs.

Some markets are more commercial and some others are more editorial. By commercial, we mean for the money. Editorial is for beautiful pictures for your portfolio and the exposure to others who buy fashion magazines.

Your "look" may be in high demand in a very small market but for you it could be highliy lucrative.

All the information about YOUR kind of market, that you work in, is good to know, so ask questions about different markets with other girls, especially experienced girls or ones with a similar look to yours who have been to other markets you haven't been to.

It is incredibly important your accountant is familiar with the kind of international work you will be doing, so they can advise you on how you can go about your business and which receipts to collect.

PARIS

Is an editorial market. Girls go there for tear sheets, which are the pictures from magazines that they then put into their portfolios.

A lot of editorials have 6 or 8 pages of fashion featuring one girl so it is a major chance to get good pictures for your portfolio and to work with people in the business who can recommend you for other jobs. Having such pictures in well known magazines will also, obviously, expose you to a wide range of readers, clients and others in the fashion business, so editorial is very important. It is especially good if the photographer is well known for great pictures, or is currently hot.

Editorial is considered creative and prestigious, especially if it is an important magazine like French Elle, Vogue or Marie France. Magazines can change their look over time with new editors, so pay attention to the ones you would like to work for, and which photographers you like, as you may visit their studio on a gosee soon! Your agency can recommend which magazines they may be grooming you for, or envision you having a chance to work for.

French magazines are prestigious to have in your portfolio as the competition in Paris is very strong, the city is expensive and difficult to live in as a foreigner and the agencies are very tough. Clients forge specific relationships and it is not an easy market, so having French tear sheets shows you have put in your legwork and have struggled with heavy competition.

Shows are also an important part of this market and can have a major effect on raising your profile as a model. (Getting your face known) The shows are seasonal and your agency can tell you when the castings start. Shows are seen all over the world and the photographs and television coverage can do a lot to increase your exposure, especially if you can land a show for a famous designer.

Day rates, or the amount you get paid per day, can be low for shows. If you are new or unknown, it can be a couple hundred Euros or less, depending on the magazine or the show. Agencies in Paris will charge you 20% of your daily rate in commission, and regularly withold income tax of up to 30% or more if you are a foreigner, which doesn't leave much over for the rent. Advertising jobs can pay almost 3 times the amount than in some other countries, but the competition is fierce and unless you have a lot of good tear sheets in your portfolio or are a shooting star, it is best not to expect too much from a market that is notoriously difficult. Try to enjoy yourself and learn from the experience as Paris can really teach you a lifetime of lessons in a short period. With so much of your money being subtracted before you even see it, Paris is not always a money market. Most French girls have agencies in other countries to supplement their income and to take advantage of the prestige of their tear sheets.

MILAN

Is also an editorial market but is much easier for mainstream girls to get great pictures for their portfolios, as there is a healthy testing community of photographers there. A "test" is what people call a production that is basically internally generated by either photographers or hair & makeup people or stylists. No one gets paid; they donate their time as a team so everyone can get photographs for their portfolios. It is also a good way for hair & makeup people and stylists to introduce themselves to photographers they haven't worked with before. Working without a client and a briefing to stick to, means everyone can be more creative and experimental with their ideas. The purpose is to come out with great images for everyones portfolio though, so try not to let it be too free and crazy. It is also a chance for the model to impress all of the others who may be able to suggest them for a job in the future

Testing is a good way to build your portfolio but also to make contacts and forge friendships. Your agency will be able to put you in contact with photographers they know that regularly test with their models or you may meet a photographer on a gosee that may suggest doing a test. Be sure to see some of the previous pictures the photographer has taken, or clearly discuss the concept of the test so you understand what kind of pictures he/she intends to take. Make a note of the photographers name and ask your agency what kind of reputation he/she has.

Shows are just as important in Milan as Paris for a model, for all the same reasons. Only some of the most talented people are involved back stage in the shows and they do the shows all over the world, travelling in teams to New York and Paris, so it is an incredible opportunity to meet the really talented creative people behind the looks! There is also a lot of waiting around time at shows so bring a book, your knitting or your ipod. Take the chance to meet other models or hair & makeup artists, make travelling companions or just meet a new, wonderful friend.

It is also much easier to have a good time in Milan. Agencies work together with nightclubs so drinking and eating for free is much easier for models and is practically expected of you, from

your agency there. There is a lot of reference to "clients" when talking about evenings out and there are plenty of opportunities for smart models to eat and meet others in Milan for little or no money. Milan is much easier and social, compared with Paris, the agencies there take 20% in agency fees but often withold tax as well, whether you have papers to work there or not. The rates are not as high as Paris and the agencies are not as tough, but expect some social participation. It is not compulsory but on the other hand be smart. (see chapter on drinking/drugs pg 94)

HAMBURG / MUNICH

Germany was considered for a long time a money market and although it is in transition, it is still considered a money market. Although friendly and accommodating, German clients can be very disciplined and rigid. There is much less stress placed on social involvement but German clients will always expect to get what they paid for and are known for their directness and professional attention to details. This includes being punctual, attentive to the work schedule (i.e. not talking on the phone when you need to be on set) as well as happy and quiet, even if you don't understand the language.

The editorial in Germany is not widely respected as being either fashionable or creative and therefore it pays quite handsomely compared to other markets. Germany has always had a healthy catalogue clientele, with several large catalogues producing throughout the year. The advertising rates in Germany are not as high as in France and the model agencies will take 25% commission fees plus another 19% of that commission fee, for sales tax. You will be responsible to pay your own tax and will be asked by your agent to fill out and sign the forms necessary. Some clients withold income tax from foreign models so keep this in mind.

As a well-known money market, Germany is highly competitive and can be flooded in summer, as models flock in to earn money in August, as Paris and Milan are closed for summer holidays. This is a great opportunity to see clients, enjoy the summer in a beautiful city such as Hamburg and establish yourself with a few German clients.

LONDON

Is one of the worlds most recognized and vibrant fashion centres. Incredibly creative, it also has a thriving economy and rates paid in English pound can really put you in the money, but remember it is also an incredibly expensive city. Most agents will expect you to live in London if you want to take a serious crack at the market. The work is diverse, the market competitive but incredibly creative, free and exciting. This is the perfect place to explore your own fashion style as people experiment without fear of feeling conspicuous.

Once again there is a large variety of work including shows, but as one of the most recognized creative fashion markets, the variety of work itself will almost guarantee you a chance at work. An important or influential agent is a must if you want to make the most out of this market.

Agents in London will charge 20% commission on your day rate, and may, or may not, withold income tax, depending on which country you come from. Remember- everyone must pay tax!

SYDNEY

Has been a favourite destination of models as the quality of tear sheets and the creative standard is quite high. It is still considered a small market but is a perfect place to have a working holiday to work on your portfolio, especially if you are just starting out. The economy there is doing well and agencies will charge 20% commission fees but again, may withold income tax. This is common practice there, even for residents. The agencies are professional but like everyone there, they are easy going and relaxed.

There is not a lot of catalogue work but this market appreciates commercial as well as special looks. It is best to choose an agent before arriving as they can create a buzz for you before you arrive and suggest the best time for you to be there for work. There is no distinct seasonal work but most magazines will take holidays over the Christmas and New Year period, as it is summer there, and will not be back in the office until the beginning of February in some cases. Generally Australia is considered an editorial market.

NEW YORK

Well, it is not called the big apple for nothing! This is a huge and diverse market, which can springboard your whole career. The time you put in to New York will be rewarding in several different ways. As America's economy is the largest and their consumers insatiable, it is not only a huge editorial, but also a huge advertising market. All of the best models in the world have cracked New York and gotten their breakthroughs there but the market is especially dog eat dog and not much time is wasted on those who have the potential, but are struggling a little. Be sure you are strong, independent and fit for this market. Agencies will take 20%. Income tax may be witheld, check with your Agency there. Be ready for this market, it is not one to cut your teeth on!

HOW LONG TO STAY IN A CITY

This question is best answered in general terms, as there are a lot of variables to consider. Firstly, how far are you away from another city or market? If you have been in a city doing gosees for 2 or 3 weeks and haven't had one option it is best to move on to another city and do gosees there. Your agency will be able to help you understand why you are not getting any bookings and will understand if you ask them to arrange some gosees in another city (in Germany for example you may see clients in Hamburg as well as Munich) Some clients are in other cities and it can be worth it especially if it is a big client and the agency feels strongly that the client would book you if they met you personally.

Another thing to consider is, if you are having fun and can afford to stay for a while. If after 3 or 4 weeks it is still fairly quiet, it is wise to leave so you can use the time to do gosees in another market, or go home to save some money.

WHICH MARKET IS FOR YOU

Although modelling is a fun job, it is a business and you should consider which market would be best for you and your business. Consider not only the big markets but also some of the smaller ones. It is good to spread yourself thin in this business, to see where your looks and personality are appreciated and where you will be happiest.

Some markets may be small but quite lucrative. Sweden and Denmark are small markets but have very well received tear sheets and pay well due to the exchange rate of the Euro. Athens and Barcelona are also small markets but a good place to work on your book (another name for your portfolio) and earn some money while enjoying the culture. It really depends if you are just starting out or need to work on your book due to a new hair colour or cut.

If you see yourself as strictly commercial and want to change your look to generate some new interest, it is always best to consult your agency before changing your look too drastically. Your agency are not your parents, who will forbid you to do something crazy because they don't like it, they are your business partners and will advise you based on their experience and their judgement of what will happen financially.

Of course they may be leaning to the conservative side of their judgement, but that is because they know most clients don't like huge changes. If you feel you have nothing to lose anyway, then discuss it with the head booker or the owner of the agency. He or she deals with the clients everyday and will have several alternatives for you to think over. The final decision will be yours, as it is your look and your livelihood but it is extremely important to discuss such things with your business partner.

Generally, it is best to get into an editorial market as clients can see a variety of looks you can be perfect for. Commercial and advertising clients have very little vision when it comes down to it, sometimes they will feel safer if they can see a picture in your book which is exactly the kind of look they have in mind for their job. Bear this in mind when you decide to do a test. What kind of clients are you looking to attract and what exactly is it they are looking for? Better yet, what asset do you have, that you think they need? Your smile? Your lips? Your fantastic legs, skin or chameleon like characteristics? Can you make clothes look good? Consider all these things and then it could be up to you to PAY a testing photographer to shoot exactly what you need, to attract the kind of clients you want to work with. Again, discuss your "look" with your agent. An agent in Germany will probably err on the conservative side, as it is a commercial market, whereas an agent in Paris may recommend something more dramatic.

Being distinctive in an editorial market is the whole point, but remember to consider your features and do something to compliment and strengthen your look.

Above all make sure you do your homework with a photographer that you choose for a paid test, if you are paying. Some photographers assistents can be really talented and some just think they are. Ask to see their portfolio, or ask a photographer you get on well with, if they test, but be polite and humble, you never know...

STUDIO PROTOCOL

Working in the studio for the first time can be a bit daunting as I am sure you remember.

Having been on gosees you should be quite comfortable with the atmosphere, but there are a few things to remember when you are at work. Firstly, it is normal for people to be watching you all day, so get used to it. Try to always arrive at least 10 minutes early. This immediately lets your team and client know you take your job and responsibilities seriously.

In England some people shake hands when they first meet on jobs but in mainland Europe it is common to kiss on the cheeks. Do what ever feels most comfortable. Some people will do both so just don't be surprised if strangers sudenly pull you in for kisses on the cheeks. The French usually kiss 3 times; the Italians and Germans do it twice, one on each cheek. It isn't necessary to actually put your lips on their cheeks; just touching your cheeks together is enough. Be sure to greet your team warmly in the morning, as you will be working closely with them all day.

Hair and makeup artists have a limited amount of time allowed for them to work on you, so always arrive with clean hair and face. It doesn't matter if you think your hair looks fuller with mousse in it or not, you are on a job and the hair stylist has something to deal with any condition your hair is in. Already having heavy product in your hair or dirty hair means time is wasted in the studio washing it, before they can even start. Even if you didn't take all your makeup off after the party last night, or think you MUST wear eyeliner on the train to the job, it is a sign of respect to arrive with a totally clean face (take a Q tip to clean between your upper and lower lashes completely). Makeup on your face either from the night before or not properly removed before a job is just wasting the makeup artists' time. Show your team the respect they deserve and they will respect you in return.

Put your things in the makeup room or area somewhere where they will be out of the way. Don't bring a lot of money or valuables with you to your job unless you don't trust them to be left where you are staying.

Turn your mobile phone off or on vibrate. Your agency knows where you are and will call on the studio line if they need to speak to you urgently or can't reach you on your phone. Check your messages when you have a break, but otherwise concentrate on your job. Photographers can get really irritated by ringing phones if they have the feeling they have a great shot and you suddenly lose your concentration due to your ringing phone. Silly ring tones can also be really distracting. Clients have been known to complain to agencies that models were on the phone half the day so restrict any calls to absolute emergencies and don't explain to others why the call was so important. You may think it was important but it is NOT to them.

Be helpful, courteous and quiet while the makeup artist and hair stylist works on you. It takes almost as much concentration to have your makeup done as it does to do it, so concentrate on what your team is doing and think along with them. Ask the makeup artist if it is "ok" to drink from the glass or smoke, as some makeup artists can be quite annoyed if they have done a special job on the lips and you wreck it just before the picture. Often there will be straws or they will say it is fine and will touch it up before shooting. Don't touch or play with your hair or rub your face after the makeup and hair is done. This can be really frustrating to the makeup and hair artists. If it is in your way ask them to pin it away while you eat or change.

Don't chew chewing gum or candies while on the set. It is not the job of anyone to take the gum out of your mouth and put it in the garbage and you can't stick it behind your ear, in your hand, on your shoe or under your tongue without being distracted by it.

When finished with your outfit hang it back on the hanger or hand it directly to the stylist if they say not to hang it up. This way you can never be criticized for being sloppy or undisciplined. Never do anything to give anyone an excuse to criticize your professional attitude. This includes rolling your eyes, making faces or looking angry. Even if the person you did it towards didn't see, someone else will and they will judge you as immature or bad tempered. Both are bad traits for a model to have.

Try to be as charming and happy as possible. People always love charming and happy people. They are a pleasure to work with and you never get tired of them.

Listen carefully to the client/photographer if he or she is explaining something to you. If there is something you don't understand, ask. This shows you are interested in getting it completely right. Even if you do get it, ask the client/photographer if it is right, what you are doing and if they would like more smiles or less intensity to your look or what ever it is they want. The client/photographer will be impressed that you are so willing to do what is necessary for the picture. If there is something uncomfortable, distracting or hurting you concerning your outfit just look at the stylist and make a facial gesture for them to to come and help you fix it, don't call out to them or make a fuss. If they are not there, do the gesture to the hair or makeup artist. They will go to the stylist and bring them to the set. Try to be as cool as you can. Follow direction as best you can even if two people are saying two different things. If you are really at a loss as to what to do just laugh a little and ask the photographer what he wants you to do. He will then solve the problem with the art direction.

STYLISTS

These are the people responsible for getting the clothes and accessories to the set and deciding how the look is put together. They are often overworked and stressed by the time they arrive for the shooting, but they can have a lot of power with the client. If you are shooting for a magazine, they ARE the clients!

As creative people of vision they often have that glazed over look of assessing whether the look is right as it is, or needs something else, when they are helping you to dress. Be patient with them and help them if you see they are unsure by doing something you might do in front of the camera, on the set. This can help them decide if the outfit is right. By you getting in character, they can visualize it easier.

Some fabrics crease and wrinkle easily so be aware of bending over to do up shoes etc. Ask the stylist if you should bend to do up the shoes, if you are unsure. Try to think ahead by putting on pantyhose and shoes first, if possible. After shooting an outfit, be sure to treat the clothes with respect even if you are in a hurry. Hang the clothes back on the hanger or drape them carefully over a chair or best of all, hand them directly back to the stylist. Stylists have a special relationship to the clothes and accessories and have poured over them for hours, so when you disrespect the clothes, the stylist may see it as disrespecting them or their job. Try to see the clothes as an extension of the stylist and the stylist will always like you. Stylists work hard to make you look your best for the picture and may also recommend you for more jobs, so be sure to show them you appreciate their effort. Thank them before you leave the studio for the day. It is a small gesture but it is always appreciated.

HAIR AND MAKEUP ARTISTS

Always try to get along well with the makeup artist and hair stylist. They can be some of the warmest and funniest characters on the set and can cover for you if something goes wrong. If you need an extra minute or have a special problem like not feeling well or having issues in your personal life, they are the one to turn to. If you don't know them at all, it is not necessary to go into details with them, but they will help you out if you need it. If you are being melodramatic they will probably tell you that too, so rely on them as you would a friend, and they will usually help you out. Especially if they have worked with the photographer before, they

can help you with tips of how he or she is to work with and if there is something special to be careful of. Often if the photographer has a short fuse or is well known for certain behaviour they can tip you off. If the photographer is known for a famous story they did for a certain magazine, the makeup artist will know and tell you of his genius work so you can prepare for the experience.

Always thank your makeup artist, and tell them you hope to work with them again soon. This leaves them feeling like you have appreciated their work and personal support. Makeup artists and hairdressers are like mothers and brothers, so feel free to make them feel good for their constant efforts. If you did not feel so warm with them, thank them warmly anyway, as they will feel a twinge of regret if you remain charming up until the end.

PHOTOGRAPHERS

When the photographer comes to chat to you, give him/her all the charm and attention you can without being obvious. Photographers feel they have a special relationship with models as, through the lens it is just you and them. They sometimes will want to get to know you better so they can get the best performance out of you and sometimes they like to flirt a little to get the energy flowing between you. Sometimes this is just as much for the photographer as it is for you, so if you can let him / her know you are ready, willing and able to give them all your attention and talent, it will reassure them. It will benefit you in the long run as it will also put you in the mood to give all you can for a great picture.

Your photographer is the most important person on the set for you. You will take all your direction from him or her, as usually the client or art director will have briefed the photographer on what they want for the picture.

The difference between a picture and a great picture is art, and that is the energy between the characters. Whether it is artist and canvas, or model and photographer it is the special energy on the day that makes a great picture. So put yourself in the flow and enjoy the experience. Relax and be open and attentive to the personality of the photographer, he or she will lead you.

It is important not to get over excited and to keep the energy controlled and focused on the job. This may sound a little strange, but once you feel yourself able to ignore distractions or the giggles and focus yourself back onto the job you will know what is meant by staying in the flow.

Always give your utmost to show the photographer you are willing to do everything to get the picture he/she wants. Always be attentive!

PHOTOGRAPHERS ASSISTANTS

The assistant to the photographer is usually quiet and concentrated on his job and the photographer. You can sometimes take your lead from the assistant, as they are often fine tuned to the photographer, especially if they have been working together for a long time. If you are chatting with them and they suddenly are quiet you know that you too must pay attention to the others or get back to work, and not be too loud so the others can concentrate. They should be respected for the hard job that they often do.

EDITORS

Editors can work on a fulltime or part time basis for one magazine or several different ones. They will be responsible for the concept and styling of the picture and the photographer may consult with them if there is a decision to be made on the job. You should treat the editor as your

client, as essentially they are the boss and will be answerable for the decisions made on the day. These women/men are normally very strong and clear about what they want in the picture as they have been preparing the concept for some time and have been thinking about the concept and direction they want the pictures to take. If you are not clear about the concept or what exactly the editor wants in the picture it is best to ask her/him directly. Call her by her first name unless everyone else refers to her as something different. People always like to hear their own name, so remember to call her by name when you speak to her. Listen to her closely and ask questions if you are not clear. If the concept is sounding very loose and you feel a bit confused, but you think it is too embarrassing to ask any further, just do what you feel is the right thing. If the photographer feels it is not really what he / she wants, they will let you know, then you will have a second chance to ask about the concept.

When a Polaroid is taken, or you see the first digital images, wait until the others comment about whether they like it or not. If they like it keep working in the same direction. If the editor wants something different from you, she will either ask you directly or she will ask the photographer, to ask you. Don't be offended by this. Very often photographers prefer to have the main contact with the model as they like to establish a feeling of trust and closeness which enables them to see a special part of your personality. If the editor is very involved with you but is distracting you while you are shooting it is always best to focus your attention only on the photographer. It is wrong for you to look at the editor constantly when the photographer is shooting pictures (unless he asks you to look somewhere else) If you don't like the pictures it is

best not to comment at all. Do your job as a professional, be in a good mood and do not sulk or shrug your shoulders if someone asks if you like the pictures. You are not expected to understand or like all the pictures that are taken of you. Being charming is ABSOLUTELY part of your job and if your taste is wildly different to what you find yourself in the studio shooting, treat it as a learning experience. Understanding the process of being creative in the fashion business will always be helpful to you, whether you understand and agree with what one team or magazine does or not. Just as in life, learning from the mistakes, or the bad experiences can be a much faster way to learn than only having the positive and wonderful ones.

CLIENTS

Clients can take many forms and it can be quite hard to generalize but the best way to handle your client is as an editor but with the utmost respect as you would the parents of your new posh boyfriend. Once you get to know the client they will let you know how formal or informal your friendship can be. Always remember this is the person who will have a big say in whether you are booked again or not, so be charming and professional around them as you are with the others.

ART DIRECTORS

Often Art Directors will talk a lot about the layout, this is the format in which the pictures and text are put together on the page. They are often the creative imagination behind the concept of the job, therefore they will direct the photographer and may also direct you, although often they will leave that up to the photographer. They can also be confusing, because they want everything in the picture so it will appeal to everyone who sees it. Be prepared if that happens.

ON THE JOB TROUBLE?

It happens very rarely but sometimes the job can have a hiccup. It can be something they want you to wear that is completely see-through that you don't feel comfortable with or the client/ photographer doesn't like the hair and makeup or there is a technical problem with the lights or the camera. In all of these situations, whether you are involved or not it is best to say as little as possible about it and stay absolutely cool. Be attentive, so you know what's going on but have no opinion about it at all. That way you will not be quoted as saying this or that and they will wonder at how cool and professional you are. If it is something you have cleared with your agent but the photographer or client is still insisting, be firm and polite. If any discussion arises, tell them pleasantly you will just check with your booker. Call your agency and let them handle it, that is their job and they can handle it easier than you.

If it is a see through dress and you are not comfortable with it or don't do that kind of work and you have discussed it with your agency you can just insist on keeping your skin toned underwear on. If it is not "ok" with the others, call your agency and let them speak to the client. Be polite, patient and courteous with the client / photographer but you have a right to stand your ground about your own body.

If it is the hair and makeup that is the problem, it is not your responsibility, so it is best to say nothing. If you feel it is beautiful and you like it, try to pose in the way you think you would in the set, so the client or photographer can see how it may work in the picture. If they still insist it should be changed and the stylist is upset do NOT join in on any criticism of anyone. Tell the stylist you loved it and try to cheer them up by making a joke or changing the subject.

With all other problems that do not directly concern you, it is best to have no opinion at all. Even if privately you are pressed by the hair and makeup or stylist, still insist it makes no difference to you or better yet, say nothing and just smile. ALWAYS avoid saying something anyone can quote you on. If you feel something has gone wrong and you feel it has something to do with you or you don't know, call your agent and talk to them immediately so they know first hand from you, what the situation is from your side before they have to talk to anyone else about it. There is nothing worse for your agency than to be blindsided by an irate client / photographer.

If the photographer is taking his flirting a little too far and you feel unsure of yourself in the situation you can always ask the hair and makeup artist to help you out on how to handle the uncomfortable situation. Be diplomatic and lighthearted about it. The hair and makeup artists are used to backing up girls stories so don't be nervous to ask. If you just feel a bit unsure of yourself, but feel it is a bit uncool to say anything, you can just smile and say nothing. That is always a safe bet!

CASTING LINES

Dressing the part for castings and gosees to blow your competition out of the water

THIS PAGE Beauty castings need an outfit that compliments your skin tone and has an accent or a feminine detail to add interest.

THIS PAGE Changing your look on the run between castings can be as easy as adding a scarf or a baseball hat. Use accessories to set the mood of your outfit.

PREVIOUS PAGE Castings for music videos are a chance for you to show you are not afraid to be taken notice of. Choose clothes with plenty of personality and add funky accessories like cool glasses and a hat just to turn up the volume.

THIS PAGE Going to castings and gosees needs alot of stamina. Wear comfortable shoes, layer your outfit and bring accessories, water and a snack incase you have to wait at a busy casting.

THIS PAGE Lingerie and beauty castings can be nerve wracking. Bring your bikini, wear your best matching lingerie and be sure to shave and moisturize yourself well ahead of time.

NEXT PAGE If you have a casting for a show, you will need to bring the attention to your great walk, and what better way than by showing a bit of leg. Bring heels with you and wear a longer jacket for walking in the streets.

THIS PAGE   Trying to dress to seem a little older can be a tricky thing if you are quite young. It is best to wear a strong classic piece with no or very minimal accessories. Make a sophisticated statement with strong sunglasses and a womanly handbag.

AGENCIES

Your agent will be your business partner and your doorway to meeting your clients.

The relationship you have with your agent will be one of the most important relationships in your business life, so be sure to nurture and handle this relationship with honesty, commitment and reverence.

Your agent has a business to run so don't waste their time with pettiness or hysterical behaviour.

Showing your agent respect will bring you respect in turn. When they see you are willing to go out of your way to be helpful, courteous and professional, they will have confidence in supporting you even when times become a little tougher. As much as your looks may MAKE you a model, your personality and ability to work hard and remain professional under pressure will be the true test of your character. It will also assure you success and longevity in a tough and competitive business. Don't let anyone give you the impression modelling is easy or isn't character building. It is stressful both physically and emotionally and when you are a long way from home your agent can be the only one to turn to if you need help.

Having said that, your agent is not your mother or the bank, so respect any favors they may do as favors, not something you are entitled to. Some agents will offer you "pocket money" between 80 and 100 Euros a week but this will later be subtracted from your earnings so don't spend it lavishly. The agency will only allow you this favor as they know you are broke, but have confidence you will work.

Building up debts at your agency can restrict you from travelling out of the city so try to be back in the black as soon as you possibly can. This will also put you in a positive state of mind and your agent will note that you are responsible, for future reference.

Your "Mother Agency" is the agency that initially discovered or first signed you. This agent will feel the closest and will probably be the most protective of you so it is really important you feel close and secure with them. They will be the ones who will help you to decide on which foreign agents you should have and what your career strategy should be. Sometimes, even if your mother agent or a scout discovered you, another agent may be the one who can promote you and give your career real takeoff, so it may be best for you to spend most of your time where you work the most.

There are many people working within an agency with varying responsibilities and seniority. Try to speak to the right people and ask your questions to the people who have the authority and experience to answer your questions. If you are unsure, ask whom you should speak to about your bookings or day rates or problems on a job. By the time you are up and working you should know everyone working at your agency and their responsibilities where you are concerned.

As in life, sometimes you are asked to do things that you may prefer not to do or have situations that become disappointing. It is up to your individual personality and your maturity, how you deal with these situations. Becoming openly frustrated or aggressive will show your agent you may be too immature to deal with more important or responsible situations or assignments. The agency is constantly tracking your ability to handle yourself and your responsibilities so bear that in mind when speaking to them. For example: If an assignment turns out to be cancelled at the last minute, you must accept it as part of how the business works. Naturally you can be really disappointed, but being able to accept the decision without frustration, tears or withdrawal, will show your agent or booker that you are mature and prepared for difficult eventualities. You may put the phone down and have a freak out to yourself, but your ability to collect yourself and get on with things will prove you understand how things work and you are ready for the next situation that can just as quickly arise. You are certainly entitled to say how disappointed you are but keep your tone even and move on without obsessing about it.

You may also become angry or frustrated that your agent has handled a situation differently than how you were expecting. It is really important for you to keep your composure. It is fine to be disappointed and you may openly express that you are disappointed, but remember to do it in a mature and respectful way. Your agent or booker is not your emotional punching bag. They will respond to you in a more positive way and be encouraged to try to make you happy if you treat them with respect in the face of difficulty. If you remain charming and even-tempered, it will get you further in your business ventures than creating a reputation for yourself as being difficult or hysterical. If you feel unable to keep your emotional control, try looking at the situation differently than you do. For example, imagine you are the client or your agent. When you feel yourself getting "hot" try to behave in the exact opposite way than you normally would, and see if you cannot achieve the exact same objective, without the negative behaviour. Practise makes perfect.

If you have a situation that could affect your future bookings such as a job that will require you to have your hair cut and coloured, be sure to discuss the details in person with the head booker or someone else who will take responsibility that exactly the amount cut off and the colour discussed will be done on the day of the job. Get the decision in writing if necessary.

Try to remember it is also no picnic for your booker to call you with bad news either. Making it into a nightmare experience for your booker or agent does not put you at the top of any "favorites" list. Try to establish a professional attitude as soon as you can, as it will make the communication between your agency and yourself flow easily and will be conducive for a mutually respectful, trusting and long-lasting relationship.

HOW TO CHOOSE AN AGENCY

Whether you are already an established model or just starting out, choosing an agent is always a tricky job. The best approach is to really do your homework. Look at the web sites of the agencies that you know. Pay attention to the type of models they have on their books and the kind of tear sheets and jobs the models have in their portfolios. Most professional models will not say anything negative about their agencies openly and if they do, it is cause for you to suspect their professionalism.

Once you have made a list of three or four agents that you feel could be appropriate for you, call to arrange an appointment. Bring your current portfolio with you to the appointment and in a relaxed and clear way explain why you are unhappy with your current agent without going into any long stories or critical examples. You may feel it is necessary for you to explain yourself but the new agent will find it unprofessional and negative on your part. It is best to concentrate on how you would like the situation to be in the new agency and ask questions of the person meeting with you. You can ask whether they have many girls from your country in the agency and what kind of clients they predominately work with, what day rates you could easily expect to get for a day of editorial or advertising and which direction they could imagine you would be best suited for.

All people you meet with should be polite and friendly. Ask to meet with the person who will be your booker as it is very important that you communicate well with your booker. Having a close relationship with your booker can greatly benefit your work just as having your booker think highly of you both professionally and personally, can be easily picked up by the clients on the phone.

BOOKERS

As mentioned above, having a close relationship with your booker can be of great benefit. Bookers are the ones who deal with the day-to-day business of talking to clients and photographers about you, your beauty, skills and temperament. No smart booker will say anything negative about any of the models they take care of, but all bookers will jump at the opportunity to say something positive about a model they honestly like and believe in. The clients can also hear in the voice of the booker, their honesty, enthusiasm and confidence with which she recommends them, it's natural.

Be appreciative of all the hard work your bookers put in and be sure to always thank them. Make them feel and know how valuable their efforts are to you. No one likes to be taken for granted and the bookers are individuals with feelings too, make them feel special and appreciated. This in turn will encourage them to try to make you happy.

Everyone likes to be rewarded for doing a good job and pushing hard for you, so remember their birthday and treat your booker like a queen/king at every chance you get. It will be you who will reap the benefits.

Some bookers can be quite blunt and impatient. Always take into consideration they have other stresses and problems to deal with besides yours, so be patient and understanding. Remaining calm and charming in tense situations will show your booker the level of professionalism you are capable of, but if the situation continues, or you feel personally offended, ask to have a meeting with your agent or the head booker and try to rationally come to the root of the problem. It could be something like a simple misunderstanding or communication problem. Be clear and even toned without sounding accusing. Sometimes it can be just as simple as you`re more familiar with the way New Yorkers get straight to business, and the booker is used to a little friendly chit chat during conversations. When it comes to weight loss and other issues that might bug you remember, bookers are human and may not even realize they are hitting you in a sore spot.

It is not uncommon for a booker to mention your weight everyday or in negative ways that might hurt your feelings however, they are trying to give you information to help get bookings. Sometimes, especially in Paris where models are expected to be extremely thin, the bookers are so used to harping on to girls about their weight, they may not even realize they are doing it. It is not in your best interests to become distracted by the behaviour of your booker. Obsessing over your weight is not the way you should react. Losing your temper or arguing about it is also not the best response. It is a well-known fact that permanent weight loss takes more than a few days. Your results will be hindered by being stressed and upset and will only escalate the

situation, so stay cool and do not play into being easily manipulated. If you are strong businesswoman, the attempt to distract you from your business and make you obsess about yourself and your weight will fail. If you do indeed need to lose a few kilos, set the wheels in motion by following the everyday diet and stepping up your exercise plan. This will be enough to have you back on track in 2 weeks or less. As looking slim and in shape is part of your job, you must take it seriously otherwise it will affect your agent's ability to sell you to the clients.

CHECKING IN

Every Agency will need you to check in with them during the day. Some Agents ask you to call once a day so they can give you details of your next days appointments, castings or jobs. Other agents ask you to check in twice a day, so be sure what your agent wants. ALWAYS be ready with a pen and paper so you can jot down the details. It is a good idea to put this info in a little book or diary so you don't depend on little pieces of paper, floating around in your bag or pockets.

PAYMENTS AND PERCENTAGES

Each agency has their own policies regarding payments and it will vary from country to country. The rules are usually not broken for anyone, as nearly everyone has special circumstances so do not be surprised if the agency refuses a request you may have for money. Many agencies will pay you two weeks after you have finished the job, minus the agency commission, tax and money you may be owing the agency. If you are not working in a country that withholds your tax, you are responsible for paying it yourself. If you are unsure, speak to the agency bookkeeper or your accountant. Payment can be made by cheque or paid into your bank account.

Agency percentages vary from country to country as mentioned in WORKING THE MARKETS. Pg. 72

- Milan is 20% (not including tax deductions)
- Paris is 20% (not including tax deductions)
- Germany is 25% (not including sales tax)
- South Africa is 20%
- London is 20%
- New York is 20%
- Sydney is 20%

There may be additional costs that can be subtracted from your income but these should be previously discussed with you so they do not come as a surprise. Taxi and other receipts from jobs must be forwarded directly by you, to the agency within days of finishing your job. Collect them carefully and include a note of your name, the name of the client and the dates of the job.

TAX ACCOUNTANT

Your agency will have their accountant or book keeper, but you will need to have your own accountant who will be able to advise you on what you need to collect to give to him /her and also to prepare your taxes for the government. It is important that you find one who is either familiar with models tax returns or who is familiar with international tax laws. You may be travelling outside of your home country for jobs, which is no problem, but as soon as you have bookings coming through foreign countries and foreign agents, you will need to be able to understand how to plan your finances. Some taxes that are withheld in foreign countries by your agent or clients will be able to be claimed back. You will need to collect the documents necessary for your accountant to do this.

BEING AWAY FROM HOME

Homesickness can be a really hard situation to deal with.

Most people suffer from it in some way or another, either mildly as feeling a bit down and misunderstood to feeling really upset and alone. Jet lag can often set it off. Try not to let it get a tight grip on you, as there are plenty of ways to snap yourself out of it. Letting yourself sink deeper and deeper into the depression of homesickness or feeling sorry for yourself for long periods of time is a sure sign of emotional immaturity and if you are unable to snap yourself out of it then maybe modelling is not the right job for you. There will be constant times of loneliness and times when you have to be away from your family and loved ones so try to keep a few plans up your sleeve to help, should you find yourself slipping into it's clutches! Bring photos or something small from home that normally cheers you up. Listen to fast music and dance around your room to it. Take a brisk walk to the gym and work out 15min more than usual.

You will find exercise the best medicine. That will make you feel really strong and good about yourself. Play computer games or watch a funny DVD with a friend or rent a DVD in your native language. Don't isolate yourself, everyone feels a bit down sometimes and it could be just one of those moments, so don't be hard on yourself. It is brave and strong to travel and work on your own, so feel proud. If you know you can get down, ask your agent to leave some numbers of other models in town, so you can chat when you get in. If you are on a trip, usually you are too busy to feel lonely and you will really appreciate the small amount of time you DO get alone! Don't sit and watch CNN all the time, the news just slowly makes you depressed. Get outside if it is daytime, explore your area, walk in a park that is close to your place or buy a magazine and sit and drink a cup of tea in a cafe. People watch. Buy yourself some beautiful flowers. Take up a new hobby like knitting or crotchet. Grab a great book and read about an exciting adventure or cook up your favourite recipe. Take a long bath and put on a face-mask. There are so many things you can do that are fun to do alone so take this time to get to know yourself and don't indulge your down mood.

DRINKING AND DRUGS

Most of you will already know your own limits with alcohol. Don't overestimate your own limits, as being honest with yourself is the first step in taking your success and future seriously. By being honest with yourself, you will soon find out what great things you are capable of achieving when you don't let drugs hinder your better judgement. As a model it is really a bad idea to drink as each drink contains tons of carbohydrates and sugars which, as you know are just empty, nutritionless calories. Alcohol is dehydrating and will lead to all kinds of complicated things happening to your body, which may result in wrinkles and inability to properly process fat. You know those old alcoholic guys with the open pores, red noses and potbellies? That's what I'm talking about.

If you must have a social drink make 2 your absolute limit. Order a tall glass of water as well, if you are a fast drinker, and always be sure not to drink on an empty stomach.

Always keep your drink within eyeshot. If you must leave your drink while you dance or go to the bathroom, ask a girlfriend to watch it for you and put it close to hers. No one will think anything of it. Milan and some places in Paris are notorious for slipping drugs into models drinks so just be aware of the possibility and have a back up plan organized with your girlfriends. Even males can be a target, as it is much easier to overwhelm and rob someone who has been drugged. It is often not obvious to the taste but if you limit yourself to two drinks and then start to feel quite drunk you will realize someone has spiked your drink. It is best to take a taxi home immediately if you start to feel too drunk for the drinks you have had. Your girlfriend should understand as you have accounted for the eventuality with each other. When you get home have at least one tall glass (400ml) of water before you wash your face and get ready for bed.

It is absolutely obvious that taking any kind of drugs these days is like playing Russian roulette. You have no idea where it has come from, how pure it is or even what it is. By now, if you have had any experience with drugs you will realize, not only is it not worth all the cloak and dagger arrangements and money spent, but if you have to take drugs to have any kind of a good time, then you are most definitely hanging out with some pretty dull people. Most models are able to have a great time without the use of drugs. They are outgoing and beautiful with the world at their feet, they can easily make their own fun, and do. Why would someone like that need drugs? If you are looking for drugs of any kind to improve your mood or to have a good time, perhaps you should look at the reasons why you are not already happy enough or are unable to have a good time without drugs? Refer to the section on diet, and happy food.

CLUBBING

As a model, entrance to most nightclubs is often free. Ask your agency about tickets or passes for the nightclubs in the city. They may need to put your name on a list at the door of the club. Try to always go out with people who you have met before and you trust. Bring enough money with you and write down the address of where you are staying in case you need to take a taxi home later, or cannot remember it. Be sure to have someone with you who you can depend on, should someone spike your drink or if you find yourself the subject of unwanted amorous attention!

IMAGING

This is what promoters refer to when trying to fill up a club with the right looking people in order to attract their intended clientele. In most metropolitan cities nightclub promoters will offer models all kinds of free drinks, entry and even food to get them into the club. Always be sure to go with friends for a great night out and order plenty of juice or water between your two alcoholic drinks! This is a great way to party on a budget but keep your wits about you. It is still possible to find yourself in a vulnerable situation!

FRIENDS

Most of us understand friends as being those close to us that we can trust. In the modelling business, as in life, you will meet a lot of great and interesting people who will feel very close to you in a short space of time. It is particular to this business that people feel very close, as they must work with you in a very intimate way, for a short period of time. Although it is indeed possible to become close to those you work with over time, don't put yourself in vulnerable situations socially with people you haven't known for very long. This may seem like obvious advice but it is best to consciously realize it may come down to the fact that you need a back up plan should "shit happen". Do not get into cars with strangers or when the driver has been drinking. Always have preparations in place in your mind in case you find yourself in a potentially dangerous situation. Weigh up benefits and risks carefully, as being in trouble in a foreign country can be full of complications as you can well imagine! It is not about being paranoid it is about being intelligent, independent and prepared. You are the one responsible for your safety, comfort and well-being. You are out in the big wide world and will need to think for yourself and stay on your toes, to be sure you will have nothing but fun and great memories!

DANGERS

Although you may feel like the big wide world out there is full of unknown dangers if you haven't travelled before. Or if you are young, your parents may have become worried at the prospect of you leaving home alone to go on a job in a foreign country. The truth be known,

going on an assignment with a client or magazine can be one of the safest, most enjoyable ways to travel, besides getting up early and having to work all day. You do not have to book hotels or worry about car hire or any other details of your trip, it is all taken care of by the client, production team and agency. You are travelling around together during the day working and usually meet together in the evening for dinner either in the hotel or at a place decided by someone else, so all you need to do is relax and be charming company!

If you have time off on your job either for bad weather or other reasons, your team will let you know if you should stay prepared to jump to work at the drop of a hat. In which case you will need to stay at the hotel or nearby, and with your phone charged and on so someone can reach you. Best way to make your client or photographer super angry with you? Wander off without telling anyone where you are going without any phone or means by which they can reach you. Even just wandering off without asking if it is ok to do so is not done. The client has paid well for your time, so respect their wishes even if you saw a great bag in a store and you just MUST have it, you must do as the client asks.

Travelling alone into foreign countries can be tricky sometimes, if you are not familiar with the language or local customs, but even THEN you have your Agency there who will help to put you in contact with other models from out of town. Maybe even from your home country. Better yet, go together with your booker to a night out where other models and bookers will meet up for a drink or dancing. Be happy and sociable but careful not to come off as too clingy if you are feeling a bit homesick. Just casually mention you have been feeling a bit homesick and laugh it off. No matter how casual your referrence, they will get it.

Foreign countries are just another place, so suck up the culture, Just keep your wits about you!

PACKING FOR A TRIP

If you are going to a warm tropical location it is usually pretty easy to pack, ...

... but remember what the local customs may be and bring things that aren't too see through or provocative. Photocopy a few copies of the list on the next page and for each trip, fill in the blanks and add things so you don't forget anything you may need. You should try as hard as you can to pack light, as you will be the one carrying the bag. Be aware of your baggage limitations for flights. If you are only going for 1 or 2 days you should easily be able to only have carry on luggage of around 5 or 6 kilo. Some handbags are big enough to use as a carry on but be sure to edit out the things you don't need and things that are not allowed in carry on luggage such as scissors, tweezers, metal tail combs and anything else that is metal and pointed. (This can also be a harmless things such as hair clips) More than 100ml of liquid is also not allowed.

Be aware of the clothes you favour and bring tops that can dress up jeans a bit, should your team like to visit a nice restaurant in the evening or if the hotel is a bit swish!

Obviously don't forget to include your normal model bag and dot bag (see following chapters) You will need underwear for the amount of days you are gone plus 4 extra pair of undies just incase you shower twice / decide to stay an extra day or don't want to wash out panties. You may decide to have a toiletries bag permanently packed so you don't have to raid the bathroom for deodorant, shampoo, conditioner and razors each time. Be sure to replace the used items immediately when you get back to your base so you don't have to try to remember before the next trip. A LOT can happen between now and then. Be prepared so you feel cool and collected, should you get a surprise last minute trip. Pack a few sample sachets of body cream, body scrubs or perfume samples to cut down on space. A trip can also be one of the few occasions you have time to really soak in the bath and pamper yourself, so you may need to bring along a face mask, your nail things or some other extras to use while you get the chance, if you can pack them in your checked luggage.

When travelling on flights wear soft, comfortable clothes without belts or a lot of jewellery. Even high top sneakers such as Converse high tops can take longer at airport security, so keep anything that will slow your progress through security down to absolute necessities.

GENERAL

- ◯ Passport / Ticket / Job details, contact addresses and phone numbers
- ◯ Panties for_____ days plus 4 = _____ total
- ◯ Mobile phone charger plus power adapter if necessary
- ◯ Alarm clock (unless you use your mobile as an alarm)
- ◯ Bikini
- ◯ Jeans
- ◯ Tops
- ◯ Sarongs
- ◯ Flip-flops / Boots / Sneakers
- ◯ Socks, _____ pairs
- ◯ Pyjamas / oversized T shirt
- ◯ Cosy track pants
- ◯ Good book
- ◯ Music / ipod / Headphones / Charger

TOILETRIES

- ◯ Toothbrush and toothpaste / Tooth floss
- ◯ Hairbrush / Hair dryer (some hotels have dryers in the rooms or you can ask for one)
- ◯ Shampoo / Conditioner
- ◯ Body brush (try the brush mitt from body shop)
- ◯ Shower gel (try Eucerine dry skin relief or in Germany, Eucerine Duschlotion)
- ◯ Body moisturizer (try declor moisturising body milk)
- ◯ Deodorant (use one that doesn't leave a white residue under the arm or on clothes)
- ◯ Tweezers / Nail kit
- ◯ Face moisturizer (try Dermalogica active moist or Eucerine Q10)
- ◯ Sun block (try Ultraceuticals antioxidant daily moisturiser 30+)
- ◯ Lip balm / Tampons
- ◯ Face mask / exfoliator (try Dermalogica everyday microfoliant)
- ◯ Pumice stone
- ◯ Fake tan face/body (try Nivea spray)

MODEL BAG

- ◯ Smooth t-shirt style flesh toned bra with adjustable straps (try Calvin Klein)
- ◯ Smooth flesh toned G string or tanga (try Calvin Klein)
- ◯ "Chicken fillet" bra fillers
- ◯ Shoes if you are a size 41 or larger
- ◯ Changing scarf to put over your head to protect the clothes and your makeup
- ◯ Sun block
- ◯ Body moisturizer
- ◯ Dot bag

TIME ZONES

When travelling into a different time zone it is best to try to adjust to the new time as soon as you get on the plane. Try to sleep, if it is in the middle of the night at your destination. You can use your homeopathic sleeping tablets to coax yourself into sleep. Remember to keep your eyes closed otherwise they won't work. By slowly starting to adjust to the new time you will find it much easier to adjust and won't feel exhausted when it is time to work. Read or take a warm bath to relax.

JET LAG

When you arrive from another time zone jet lag is usually the number one problem as soon as you arrive. Jet lag can work together with homesickness in a vicious cycle so be aware of this! Try to start to tune in to the new time zone before you actually leave the old one. Stay active on the day you arrive, even if you have the day free. Ask to tag along with others on go sees, just so you are not tempted to sleep all day and feel lonely at night. Go to the gym, exercise in the park or take a long bike ride or walk around your neighbourhood. You will need to burn some extra energy to exhaust yourself so you will be able to sleep at night. When it comes to jet lag and homesickness, exercise is absolutely key! Shop straight away for foods that make you happy (see page 57 for chapter on happy food) and be sure to un pack and settle yourself so you feel comfortable in your new environment. Even if it is not what you were expecting or hoping for, remember it is not forever and you are on an adventure and will successfully and professionally complete your mission!

COMFORT STUFF

Sometimes you just need a little something from home to comfort you while you are away. This can be something simple like a picture but sometimes you may feel like you really need to talk to your family and friends. This can turn into being a tricky situation for two reasons. Firstly, calling foreign countries from your mobile phone is really expensive, even sometimes if they call you, as you are also charged for part of the call. It is best to use a land line together with a cheap access number for the particular country you want to call. In england you can look on the web site below, or check newspapers.
www.moneysavingexpert.com/intcallchecker/
Also consider others may not understand jetlag or homesickness so avoid arguments.

MEDICATIONS

When you find out you may be going on a trip, check that any medication you may need while away is in your dot bag or call your doctor to arrange for a new prescription. This includes your contraceptive pill and asthma pumps. If you are also prone to tonsillitis, lip herpes or mouth ulcers when you are stressed, be sure to also include remedies for them in your dot bag. (Ferrum Phos. and L-Lysine respectively)

Usually the fact that you know you have everything in your dot bag gives you a secure and safe feeling. This alone can reduce the stress of being somewhere where you may feel vulnerable to sudden illness or pain. If you are prone to feeling over anxious about situations and find yourself often rehearsing the day in your head or worrying while lying in bed, try taking Kalms. You can buy them over the counter in London from the chemist. They are a natural herbal remedy that will not make you sleepy at all; they will help you to feel confident and relaxed.

In Germany you can try Dr Schussler salts number 5, Kalium phosphoricum (D6 is the strength). These are a homeopathic remedy for your nervous system. You may also like to try Baldrian. (only in germany)

If you are unable to find either one of these include spinach, alfalfa sprouts, sesame seeds, vegetables and brown rice in your diet.

DOT BAG

A dot bag is basically your security supply, should the unexpected happen. Normally just knowing you have your dot bag will bring a sense of calm as you know you have something for any eventuality. Obviously if you develop a fever which is uncontrolled by your homeopathic remedy contact someone in your team as you may need to see a doctor, but for most general purposes your dot bag will be there to help you out of a jam. Remember to note what you used and replace it as soon as you get home, so the next time you are off on a trip, everything will be there again for you, should you need it. Extra dots are there for your specific medication. i.e. contraceptive pill or asthma pump.

- Homeopathic sleeping tablets (if in Germany try Moradorm-S from the apotheke)
- Ferrum Phosphoricum Homeopathic cell salts (in Germany ask for Dr. Schussler salts D6) for fever, take 2 tablets every hour as soon as the fever starts, until it passes
- Four or five vitamin e oil capsules (for fast skin healing / pimples)
- Stemetil or a homeopathic equivalent from the chemist for nausea
- Zantac or Rennies for heartburn (read everyday diet)
- Compeed plasters for blisters
- Period pain killers (try Buscopan from the apotheke or chemist)
- Toothache painkillers or ibuprofen (in Germany try Tispol from the apotheke)
- Alkaline sachets (try Urea sachets) to use in case of urinary tract infections or try cranberry juice if it is available where you are until you can get to a Doctor.
- Herpes creme (try zorvirax) The fastest remedy is L-Lysine tablets from the health food store.
- Kalms (from the chemist in London. 2 tabs 3x daily or 3 tabs 2x daily) can really stop nervous worrying. All natural!
- Aloe Vera gel (heals minor cuts and abrasions from razors etc)
- Small bottle tea tree oil (use it as an antiseptic, anti fungal for the feet, for minor burns or a few drops in hot water as an inhalant)
- Anaesthetic throat lozenges (numbs your throat and tongue so you can concentrate on work, if you have a really sore throat)
- Anti nausea medication (Nux Vomica homeopathic drops)
- Headache /Asprin for fever or before long haul flights to thin the blood (1 asprin a day)
-
-
-

PLACES TO STAY / RENT

In every **metropolitan city** with a lot of models there are the usual places the agency uses to **house models.**

Model apartments are notoriously ugly, messy and sparsely decorated so if you have had experiences in living with other models in these apartments try to make arrangements for a place to stay either with friends or in a place you have stayed before. Buy a Falk plan map of each city, (or A-Z London) as they are easy to read and compact to use while on the move.

MILAN

In Milan there are apartment buildings that are regularly rented out to models. They are called residences and are normally quite expensive for what they are. Your agency will put you in touch with one or will make a reservation for you at ones they normally deal with.

The advantage of this is you can get together with a friend and rent one together so at least you get to choose with whom you live. They are normally tackily decorated but have a small kitchen and a TV. The residence will be full of other models so you will have plenty of company if you like that or not. Be sure to bring your own music.

Food and entertainment in Milan is easily accessible for models and is actively encouraged by bookers there. Evenings of entertainment where there will be a lot of "clients" are often arranged by the agency, at no cost to the models. Sometimes cars are even sent to pick you up. These evenings are usually harmless enough and can be fun if you are smart and keep your wits about you. Heavy drinking is absolutely not recommended. Go, dance, eat and have fun but remember, this is not a life style; it is just letting off steam every now and then. Milan is where all the cliché stories about fashion come from so be warned if you are young and naive.

Underground trains buses and trams will get you around the city easily. A weekly pass will cost you 9 Euro, a monthly pass is 30 Euro. You will need 2 passport photos for an ID card. The card will cost you 8 Euro. Passport photos can be done at Cardona station. Bring your passport as ID to get the card as well as the passport photos.

PARIS

There are also model apartments in Paris and they can be quite hard to deal with if you are working a lot and have been working for a while so ask your agency if they can arrange for you to rent a room in a private home.

The club scene in Paris is not so heavily emphasized in Paris and most models take their job and themselves quite seriously there. Paris will teach you a lot about the business and can be very intimidating to the inexperienced but just take things as they come there. It is a great place to learn and get the experience you will need for the rest of the world.

LONDON

Everyone knows how expensive London is and most people spending any real time at all in London will move there for a period of time, as you can't really drift in and out of London for work. Rooms can be found easily through Internet message boards and web sites. Ask your agency for help with the names of the sites they most often use or if they can connect you with someone who is also looking to share accommodation. To get started, sites like travelstay.com gumtree. com and bestroomsinlondon.com can give you some idea of what accommodation can cost in London. Use your maps to get an idea of how far out of central London some places are. Tube passes for a week will cost around 22 pound for zones 1 & 2 with an oyster card, which is a prepay travel card. Airport transport from Gatwick and Stanstead is around 14 pound one way by train but buses can be 8 pound. Rent can be around 100-150 Pound a week, look for double glazing, which is when there is double glass in the windows keeping the noise out and the heat in. Also try to get a place in zone 2 so your travel cards will be cheaper. Your agency may be able to help to get you started but it will be cheaper to rent a permanent room as long as you are earning pounds.

SYDNEY

Most places to stay will either be with private people or in a model apartment. Rents vary quite a bit there as each circumstance is different, but your agency will be able to tell you how much your weekly or monthly rent will be in the local currency. Trains don't run to all areas so buses may be the main mode of transport. Be prepared to do a lot of walking!

NEW YORK

Most agents in New York have a models apartment that they use for their girls but again, if you are wanting to spend any real time there (which you should if you are going to give it a serious shot) you will want to find a room to share or eventually think about your own place. New York is very expensive and you should allow at least 200-250 US dollars a week for rent.

There is a great network of ways people find rooms in New York. Try www.craigslist.com or the message board at your local gym. Your agency may be able to hook you up with someone else who is looking for a room mate so ask but don't pester, it's not their responsibility, they will just try to get you settled as soon as possible.

HAMBURG / MUNICH

Agents will generally put girls in a private house or sometimes a model apartment. Private apartments will be about 100 Euro per week. The city is very easy to get around with Ubahn (the underground train) and buses. If you decide to jump on a train without a ticket the fine can be 60 Euros cash on the spot if you are caught. A three-day pass will cost you 13.30 euros and an all day pass 4.65 euros. Private homes are usually quite comfortable but German landlords can be very particular about leaving lights on using too much water with long showers!

BAD HABITS

A lot of people come into adulthood with bad habits from their childhood.

It is definitely comforting to hang on to some of these habits and as hard as it is to change the habit, it will benefit your sense of maturity and your self worth. By conquering and overcoming these bad habits you will enter into a new phase of your life where you will realize your power and strength as an individual, to make things happen.

Your ability to discipline yourself will serve you well in your business and personal life and with each small step you will be carving out the life you want for yourself. Everything you do from now on should be a step towards your life goals. Set the goal clearly in your mind and make an effort everyday to move slowly but surely closer towards it.

No matter what the habit is you need to break, set the goal and make the small steps necessary to get there. Just before sleep, imagine the goal conquered and soon it will be.

NAIL BITING

This is an important habit to break as your hands will often be in pictures and acrylic nails will retard your natural nail bed, making you always dependent on fake nails.

Stick on nails are time consuming on jobs and if a client has a choice they may take a model with a less complicated routine. Using the paint on varnish that tastes bad works, as long as you realize it is not there to stop you biting your nails. It is to REMIND you, not to bite your nails because you prefer to be beautiful and earn money from fantastic jobs.

Try Homeopathic remedies for nervous conditions "Magnesium Phosphoricum D6" and "Kalium Phosphoricum D6". Be sure to include alfalfa sprouts, brown rice, sesame seeds, oatmeal, sunflower seeds and rocket in your diet.

PICKING AT NAILS

This is a most innocuous habit as it causes the cuticles to thicken, swell and bleed, creating ugly nails. Wear gloves if there are particular times when you unconsciously do it such as when watching movies or reading. Take the same remedies for nervousness as in nail biting

THUMB SUCKING

This habit is hard to break as it is simply comforting but be aware that the nail often develops a fungus that grows under the nail which retards the nail bed and makes the nail grow all wobbly. This is easy for others to notice and can be a hindrance to bookings that show hands as the thumb is almost always facing the camera. If necessary, wear cotton gloves when sleeping and use a homeopathic sleeping tablet to help you sleep without sucking your thumb.

EATING QUERKS / DISORDERS

If you find yourself eating your food alphabetically like carrots first because they start with C etc., you could be obsessing about your food. It is not unusual to be thinking a lot about food as a model, but there are some limits to healthy attitudes and it is up to you to find your perspective. Food is your friend and a healer of your body. Food gives you energy and is the fuel that drives the engine of your body. Secretly eating, binging and purging or just not giving your body the best possible fuel to work with is abuse and does need to be adressed by professionals.

This kind of abuse will only backfire on you. Eating sensibly and having your day 7 to please yourself what you have is a healthy rhythm to get into. Start today. Obsessing over your weight and yourself is introspective and it is much healthier to shift your main attention to the outside world. Get out with friends more often and read books instead of spending time mentally punishing yourself for your inadequacies. If you are having trouble managing your obsessive thoughts and behaviour, talk to your doctor and immediately turn to your list of happy food for suggestions of the kind of foods that will make you feel more in control of your behaviour. Even forcing yourself to start the day with oatmeal, seeds and nuts will make you feel much better after 2 days!

RESTLESS LEGS

This problem is quite common and can come and go. It is quickly improved by including foods high in calcium and magnesium such as alfalfa sprouts, sesame seeds, rocket, almonds, orange juice and spinach. More sleep and kalms tablets can also help. Start on the everyday diet (Pg 52) and take steps to help you to fall into deep sleep like a regular bed time.

BAD TEMPER

The true sign of emotional maturity is the ability to control your inappropriate emotional outbursts. Some girls will be young enough to think that the rest of the world can be controlled by just throwing a tantrum, but those girls and guys that truly want to make a success of their business realize it takes a lot more than good looks to be a successful model. Charm, patience, talent, discipline and timing are all an integral part of success.

If you are feeling constantly frustrated or unable to control your temper it is best to think about another profession. Your career will go nowhere if you are known for your bad temper.

SWEARING (CURSING)

This habit can be a hard one to break because these days it seems to be more and more acceptable. The difficulty lies in the fact that it is an immature mind that imagines they sound cool or tough. If an occasional profanity is uttered in extenuating circumstances, it is usually completely acceptable. It is when most of the sentence is constructed of rude words, the power of the words are lost and the mind of the listener is drawn to the character of the speaker. In other words, it is hard not to sound stupid and ignorant if every second word is a curse. For fear of stating the obvious, girls especially, do not sound tough or for that fact cool. Clients are looking for models who can project an image of sophistication, or wholeso-me good looks. Even if you still LOOK the part, clients can be disappointed and may resent a high day rate for a model which, in their eyes is common and unworthy of such a day rate. Just as disappointing as a dirty or unkept model, is a foul mouthed and rude model. It is NOT just about how you look in the picture. It is how the client likes you, and respects you to represent their company.

INVESTMENTS / SAVING MONEY

There are plenty of people who are lured into the **modelling world** with **promises of fame and fortune.**

You may be one of those who never really thought about, or even wanted to BE a model. Discovered in a nightclub or in a shopping mall with your Mum, you never really took modelling seriously, or it is something to do in your school holidays. Some of the most extraordinary careers can start out as life just throwing an opportunity your way, and you being smart or lucky enough to grasp it and for it to work out for you.

There is however one thing that rarely happens accidentally, and that is having your money work for you and having enough of it to do all the things you want to do with it. It is a sad fact that most models end their careers wondering where all the money went. Taking your career seriously enough to make the most out of it, is all about not missing opportunities. Not missing an opportunity to impress a client with your skin, nails, posture and fresh personality. Not taking for granted that this great life will last forever, and not missing the opportunity to make your money grow for you and your future. No matter what your earning potential as a model is, you will improve it for sure by polishing yourself like an expensive piece of crystal. With

With your money, no matter how much money you earn or have spare, you will increase it for sure by investing it wisely. Some of you will be earning enough money in short periods of time to almost immediately invest in property or maybe you are lucky enough to have a smart member of your family help you with investments.

If you are like the majority of models, you will be trying to scrape together the money to do all the things you need to do to keep travelling and promoting yourself to get more bookings. There can be enormous costs incurred for models just to get yourself up and running with portfolios, test shootings, travel and accommodation costs, not to mention shopping!

By understanding some simple concepts about saving and investing money you can change your feelings from being confused, stressed or uninterested in money matters, to being savy and able to find great opportunities to make your money work for you. It will help to create a secure feeling for your future. You eventually will have to think about it, so isn't it better to think about all the money you've GOT than to be asking yourself where it all went?

THE SMALL STUFF

All things start out one step at a time, the important thing is to get started. If you are thinking you have a hard enough time making ends meet, let alone having anything left over, it is time to honestly look at where your money is going and to budget yourself to save.

From country to country, bank to bank, interest rates will be slightly different but there are some common denominators we can start with that may explain why you don't have the money you want to have. Credit cards, for example.

The interest charged on credit cards is well known to be in the teens so for example if you owe 2,000 on a credit card that has 16% interest you are paying 320 in interest alone in a year! That is money that could be sitting in a savings account earning YOU interest so the first thing to do is make a bee line to pay off your credit cards or immediately find a credit card that charges less interest or even NO interest.

By checking the monthly statement to see what interest you are being charged and shopping around for a card that charges a lower interest rate you could immediately be saving yourself money. For example if you swapped to one charging 4.95% for the first six months and then went to 12.4% you would have an immediate saving of 221 and also have 6 months to pay it off. Use your credit card from then on for emergencies only and pay it off in full as soon as you can. This will help you to slowly realize that credit cards are not an unending supply of money. Use them only when you KNOW you have the money to pay them off immediately. You can also be sure if you have an overdraft at the bank the interest rate there is also in the high teens so pay attention to who is charging you for the convenience of using their money. You may find you have money in your savings but are owing money on your credit card, if this is the case pay off the card first as it is costing you money and move savings to earn you interest.

DAY BY DAY

Every day it is easy to let the small stuff mount up but as a model there will be plenty of days you won't be paying out for lunch or drinks. On the days you are running around doing appointments take a bottle of filtered still water with you so you won't be tempted by expensive designer coffees and sodas (which hinder weight loss). Pack an apple or two with you as a snack and don't let yourself get hungry during the day. A small bag of mixed nuts from home should help you if you are feeling tempted by chocolates and try to drop home for lunch if the schedule allows.

Keeping track of exactly what you are spending money on, will allow you to value how hard you have struggled and help you to get where you want to go with your finances. Don't carry this to the extreme, obviously eat nutritiously and regularly but just be aware of making sensible, price wise choices. Paying 4 Euro/Pounds for a coffee in the city is something you really shouldn't be doing, and being prepared by bringing your filtered water from home and packing a snack is just being smart. If you skipped your 2 designer coffees a day @ 3 Euro/Pounds each and lunched at home 3 days out of 5 a week saving at least 8 Euros/Pounds each time, you could be looking at a savings of 156 Euro/Pounds a month. That isn't even affecting your weekends or meeting friends for a quick bite twice a week. Just keep your wits about you when you start handing out little bits here and there, it ALL ADDS UP.

You will find, just by being a little more money conscience you can save a lot without too much compromise. Take a close look at where you spend your money by making a money diary, writting down EVERYTHING you spend money on for a week or so. You may find more going out on things that are completely unnecessary, than you think. Make changes, they will all add up!

SAVE

Knowing how to put all the little bits away for a rainy day is just part of your plan. It will make you feel good about yourself to start putting money away. Watching it grow, will keep you focused on your goals, whether it is to buy your own home or just a nest egg you can use to give yourself security for the future.

Keeping your money in an account that earns you interest will just add to your happiness because the bank will also be contributing to your nest egg. The interest rates will vary depending on the account you open and in which country, but Internet bank accounts will offer you some of the most flexible and attractive deals out there. You will need to have an account with a regular bank that has normal branches before you can open an account with one on line, but online banks offer between 2.4% and 5.95% interest on your savings with no bank charges, no minimum deposit and no fixed terms.

Check out the web site for INGDIRECT in your country. Just Google „ing direct" in your country as they have sites in the UK, Germany, Italy, France, USA and Australia. You can also check out other sites in your country that rate the banks and credit cards to see who has the lowest interest charges and who pays the highest interest. Be sure to check the terms of the accounts. Attractive offers can have a lot of restrictions or start out great and change later.

There are ways and opportunities for you to save money without tying your money up for years or months in case you need it in an emergency, but you just have to use them!

In England you can use a great site such as www.moneysavingexpert.com to get you started. This site has hundreds of great tips to help you save money. In Germany try the internet sites:geldsparen.de or kosten.de There are tons of ways to save money you just have to motivate and dedicate yourself, but it will be worth it, peace of mind and a secure future!

10 SMART WAYS TO SAVE MONEY

1. If you are often travelling, sell your car and use a car sharing company. You can join for as little as 30 Euros and book a car for as long as you might need it, a day or two for a small trip or just to take a trip to IKEA. It will cost less than 2 Euro an hour and 29 cents per kilometre. Much cheaper than owning and insuring a car! The rest of the times use your bicycle to get fit. Just use www.google.com to search for car sharing in your city.

2. Ask friends or search the internet to get competitive deals out there, you may save yourself quite a few hundred over the year.

3. Be careful to take out a set amount of cash from an ATM machine that belongs to your bank. Using a different banks' ATM machine can cost you as much as 3 Euro for the convenience. Try to budget yourself to ONLY that certain amount each week. If you have money left over at the end of the week, put it into a jar, or empty your purse of all the coins each day. At the end of 3 months take the money to the bank and deposit the money.

4. Schedule a regular amount of money to be transferred to your online interest baring account. Even if it is only 50 Euros or pounds, schedule it to be paid each week or month. If you have more money at any given time during the month you can transfer more but make a regular payment. The interest will be calculated daily and paid into your account monthly so you can watch your savings compound.

5. Sell old shoes, clothes, books and handbags online. There are a lot of people who are willing to pay money for some of the things you will never use. It's fun and you will be contacted by email when the items are sold. Be sure to use your photographic skills to make things look attractive. Especially if you are selling shoes or clothes.

6. Get into the habit of walking, using public transport or your bicycle. Keeping fit should be a natural part of your routine so use it to save money too. If you are already doing that, try to find a cheaper tariff for your mobile phone, or try to cut down the amount of time you call or text message. Every little bit you can save will add up in the end. Some tariffs offer free talk time between the same network, which can work out well if you are constantly in touch with your boyfriend or family and they have the same network

7. Go to coffee shops that have the latest fashion magazines you can read instead of buying them. This one alone will save you a fortune!! If you love to read, libraries also have all the latest books for you to read.

8. Meet friends for the movies on the discount nights. Most movie theatres have a discount night. Ask your booker, which theatres play English movies or which nights are special discount nights at movies or clubs and schedule your activities around those nights.

9. ONLY buy fashion that is on sale. You will be privy to all the upcoming trends so use your inside info, to scoop up clothes that are on sale and will fit into the upcoming trends. You will have to be quick but putting yourself on the mailing lists of your favourite stores will give you a heads up to when the sales are on. Travelling all over the world where fashions are cheaper will keep your spending down if you remember to pack light when you travel, but the golden rule is...you have to be able to pay for it immediately and cover your monthly commitments as well as your saving goals. As a freelancer money is not comming in regularly so you have to have enough to cover the unexpected.

10. Write your saving goals down. Keep them with you and tell your close family and friends so they can support and encourage you.

GETTING SERIOUSLY SMART

Certainly the hardest part about saving your money as a model is that your money is earned at irregular intervals and as a freelancer, with no single employer, you are responsible for your own health insurance, superannuation (also called retirement or 401k) plan for your old age and any other insurance needs you have.

Certainly insurance is something you should talk about with your insurance broker so if something happens to you on a job or you damage an expensive vase in a hotel, you have the insurance to cover the costs of repair, replacement or an expensive stay in a hospital. Other insurance needs will be covered for example in your superannuation, for example if you lose the ability to do your job due to an accident or illness, you need to know you are covered.

This may all sound complicated and scary but when you have your insurance agent develop a plan that is specific to your needs it will help you sleep soundly at night. You will only need to do this all once, and then you can sit back and relax knowing that you are covered for all eventualities. Covering yourself at an early age will allow you to enjoy lower premiums sooner and a tasty nest egg when you are ready for retirement in addition to your own investments.

WHAT DOES IT MEAN?

Most bad attitudes towards money and investing it, come from ignorance. If you know a little bit about what all the complicated terms mean, it may just spark your curiosity and in no time you may find yourself trawling the internet, reading books and the business section of the newspaper or picking your father`s brains for more information. Looking at a few main areas of investing, and explaining in general terms what they are and the risks involved will help you see where you are at right now and what kind of investment best suits your current money situation. All investments will entail some kind of risk, just as life itself contains some risks so you will need to also evaluate what your risk taking personality is, when it comes to investments.

It is a great pity that a lot of stuff about finance is directed at men as opposed to women, but women are slowly starting to become interested in making their own money grow for them and with the demand comes new books and web sites full of great information for women to help them get excited about their financial futures.

CASH / FIXED TERM DEPOSITS

Accounting for country-to-country variables in the interest rates, fixed term deposits are an account that has a minimum deposit, for example 5,000 and a fixed term in which the money is unavailable to you. If you decide to take the money out early you will not receive the full amount of interest, so it is best to leave the money in for the agreed period. The interest rates will vary from different banks but for this to make sense find one that pays higher interest than an online bank account as previously mentioned. To get the maximum interest leave it for the longest amount of time possible. You may choose to have the interest added to your original amount and reinvest it automatically or you may decide to have the interest paid out to you each month.

High interest earning term deposits are good if you are unsure what to do with your money or if you are saving for something specific and need

a certain amount saved. Check out your on line banking interest rates and compare them to the fixed term interest rates. You may find the online interest rates just as attractive without fixed terms and minimum deposits. Keeping your hands off the money for a fixed amount of time may be the only advantage to a fixed term in the long run!

SHARES

When you buy a share in a company you own a part of that company along with a lot of others, and your investment will grow as the company does well. The growth of your investment is paid in a dividend and is usually paid twice a year. You will be able to reinvest that dividend in shares automatically if you choose, and that is called dividend reinvestment. This means you don't have to buy more shares, as your investment grows so does your amount of shares. Alternatively you may choose to have the dividend paid into your bank account, but as with any other interest you get, you will need to declare, and pay tax on the dividend if it is paid into your account. Some dividends will already have some tax deducted from them before you get the money, this can be called „FRANKED". The company will give you a notice to say how much tax has been deducted so you will only have to pay the difference between what they have taken out and what your personal tax level is.

Dot com companies really sparked up interest in investing in shares in the late 1990s and since shares are able to be purchased online for a fraction of what brokerage fees used to cost, there are a lot of individuals investing in the stock market. Each time you buy or sell the shares it is called a trade and you will be charged a small fee for doing so.

A so-called "Bull Market" is when the price of stocks across the board are rising and a "Bear

Market" is the opposite. If you have a special interest in a specific company or you want to just play a hunch, shares are certainly risky but if you do some homework it could just be a risk that pays off. It is best to invest only as much as you can afford to lose and to sit on the shares and allow them to grow in value. There are no guarantees with shares and you can just as easily pay 20 dollars for each share and watch them dwindle away to less than a dollar when you decide to sell them.

Capital gains are the money you make from your investment. For example if you invest 200 dollars in some shares and you sell them 2 years later for 500 dollars your capital gain is 300 dollars. No matter how long you hold the shares you will have to pay tax on the money you gained from the investment. If you lost money in an investment in the same tax year (Capital loss) you can offset your loss against the gain and pay tax only on the money you made in the end.

There are many strategies to making money on the stock markets and some people make a second career out of playing the markets, but unless you are willing to research and watch the markets and specific company's' growth, it is best to leave share investment to someone who can advise you wisely.

If your curiosity is sparked and you are willing to check out the market and invest in companies you feel are sound or where you believe there is a future, such as solar energy for example, why not have a bet, just remember you should only invest an amount of money that you could afford to lose. Only invest money in the stock market yourself, if you understand it.

Build up your knowledge and confidence by reading relevant books, newspaper articles, or going to seminars. Start by checking out the business section of the newspapers or check out online market reports such as yahoo / CNN or MSN, under finance.

You will find listings of share market tables in the back pages of the business section in most newspapers. Watch a few of your favourite companies for about a month to see how the share price fluctuates. If you are further interested check out the stock exchange in your country. You may be able to get a small book from the exchange, which will explain things further for you or go to one of the seminars held to help those who want to educate themselves. These seminars may ask for a small fee but you may be the only girl there and will probably have no shortage of tutors to help you. If it all sounds too hard then stock investments may not be the best form of investment for you.

BLUE CHIP INVESTMENTS

If you like the idea of investing in stocks but don't like the idea of so much risk and research, blue chip stocks may be a better alternative. Blue chip shares, as the name suggests, are shares in companies who have a reputation for earning profits no matter if the markets are up or down. These companies have reliable growth over the long term and are less risky or volatile. It means you may have to settle for a slightly lower dividend return but you won't have the risk or need to research and educate yourself.

FUNDS

MUTUAL FUNDS Mutual funds are run by a professional fund manager. The fund has a range of investments in its portfolio, from stocks to real estate and hundreds and thousands of people invest in the portfolio collectively. The advantage is the investors can construct a diverse portfolio much cheaper than if they were acting independently. This means you don't necessarily have to know much about the investments, but you still need to make other decisions about which fund to invest in. Some funds charge commission with up front fees denoted by the A at the end of the fund name (called "front load") for example if you want to invest 10,000 and the front load is 5% you are only really investing 9,500 as the rest went to the broker or advisor. Other funds with a B at the end of their name ("deferred sales") charge you an ongoing fee attached quietly within the expense ratio, which is a fee that gets paid to the fund manager each year by the investors like you. That means you will be paying a fee each year that could be double what the front load was. Not only that, if you pull out your money before the agreed investment time, you will be stuck paying the deferred sales fee. It is best to find a no load fund with a low expense ratio. It is also important to choose a fund Manager that has a good steady long-term record, to reduce your risk. Ask questions such as how a fund has performed over a 5-year period and what was the lowest earning and the highest and why. How risky has the fund been? What does the fund own and where? Who runs the fund and how do they do it, as well as what the expense ratio is and if there are loads.

STOCK FUNDS There are many kinds of stock funds who buy stocks in companies in different sectors and in different indexes. For example growth funds buy stocks in burgeoning companies, sector funds buy in particular sectors such as technology or health care and index funds buy in an index of companies who have a record of doing well in varying financial climates.

BOND FUNDS There are varying types of bond funds too, from the safe government bond funds that may have a low yield or return but are a relatively low risk investment to high-yield bonds also known as junk bonds if you like to gamble. Keeping your tax bill down could be helped by investing in municipal funds. There

is something for every personality and money level, from a few hundred to thousands, high-risk takers to slowly and steady, but it might feel like trying to find a needle in a haystack.

INDEX FUNDS Probably one of the most boring but reliable funds. This fund is basically a bet on the market as a whole. The market goes up, your index fund will go up, when the market goes down so does the index fund.

Why is that good? Most mutual fund managers have a hard time beating the most popular broad based index, the S&P 500, which holds 500 blue chip American stocks. Look into the Stock Markets in other countries to see whose economy is doing well across the board and you will see the index funds doing well. Long term annual returns of blue chip index stocks such as the S&P 500 are about 10%, which means if you compound the interest you earn on a 1,000 investment you could end up with well over 51,000 in 30 years. Well worth thinking about eh? Some index funds will have a higher minimum investment but will charge a low expense ratio so do some comparing and find an investment made for you!

PROPERTY

Probably one of the most favourite investments as it is something you can touch and see for your money.

Buying a house or flat is an important investment and as a woman, the trick is not too get to emotionally involved with the property if it is only meant as an investment property.

It is good to buy a property that you could imagine yourself living in, but if you don't like the house because the second bedroom isn't big enough for your Mother if she came to stay, you know you are getting too emotionally involved. You will need to consider the location and the asking rents in that area as well as resale value. Investigate the growth in property prices in that area or state. You may need to buy out of state to get a better return on your investment. Choose a property which is in high demand in a popular area, for example a 2 bedroom or one bedroom, as opposed to a large house, as young people and couples are always looking for rental properties in inner city areas. A few cosmetic changes may attract better tenants and you may need to pay an agent to take care of the property for you.

A lot of things will need to be calculated into the purchase of your investment property so be aware of legal fees, stamp duties, agent fees, land taxes and bank fees before making any verbal commitment to anyone concerning your intention to buy a property. As with your other investments, educate yourself, listen to information others are willing to impart and inform yourself so you are confident about your choices. Ask family members about their house buying experience and talk to your bank so you can put in place the things you will need before asking the bank for a loan. Bank accounts that show regular deposits for your intended purchase will show the bank you are serious about saving and have a sound investment strategy in mind.

SAVING OR INVESTMENT?

As a rule if you have any debt it is best to pay off the debt before putting money away in savings. This is because the interest you have to pay on your debt will be much greater than the interest you earn on your savings. Having done that, it is up to you where you want to put your money to grow but you should try to work out a plan that allows you to choose how much money you will put into investments and how much in a savings account. The best place to start your savings is with a mini cash ISA. Each financial year the UK Government allows up to 7,000 pound to be invested and placed as cash in a

mini ISA or as a combination of cash and investments in a maxi ISA account. (this will vary in different countries so ask your accountant) This allows every tax paying resident to save up to 3,000 pounds each year, tax free, which you can save as cash and a further 4,000 in investments. The rules are complicated but worth looking into to take advantage of this tax free savings incentive, ask you accountant or check out different financial sites that can help explain how to choose the best account for you. Some sites get kickbacks from certain financial intitutions so go to web sites that give impartial advise about the best ISA accounts. I like.... www.moneysavingexpert.com/guides.phtml which gives great, simple explanations and really helps to motivate you to get into other more complicated financial information. Don't be intimidated by all this money talk, you will just need to make a good initial plan and the rest will just roll along as time passes. Before you know it you will have your money working hard for YOU!

Make your money saving plans work for your individual personality. If you know you spend too much at the supermarket, don't go shopping when you are hungry and cook up pasta sauces and soups to freeze. Also freeze sliced bread if you live by yourself or don't eat bread very often. This can help a loaf last for a month or more! You may call this your „frozen assets" but every little bit helps and this can help counteract your overindulgence at the supermarket. If you are constantly tempted by fashions, don't go shopping in boutiques, or take a friend who will help you to think sensibly about your spending. If you love beauty treatments find a salon that does cheap 20minute facials instead of long expensive ones or better yet, do your own at home with a friend. When you do get money, put it away (within the first week) into your different savings accounts and portfolios so you are not tempted. Set yourself some play money and see how long you can make it last.

MALE MO

Although it is often thought of as feminine to take a lot of care about your appearance ...

... men are slowly starting to realize that looks do count and grooming is not only important when it comes to being competitive on a professional level, but also on a social level it can certainly make you attractive to the opposite sex. You don't need to be classed as a "metro sexual" to make a few significant changes to get the right attention from the right people.

Models will need to take care of their skin and hair issues for professional reasons but as a sense of pride in your appearance, all males should pay attention to some small details if they want to get admiring glances, and let's face it, who doesn't?

THE BASICS

UNDERARMS   No matter how much of a tough macho guy you may be, body odour is totally unacceptable. For models it is especially intolerable as you are wearing clothes that do not belong to you and can often be worn later by others, so personal hygiene is priority number ONE. If you find you have a tendency to sweat nervously try a few different combination anti perspirant / deodorants until you find one that works for you. There are several different active ingredients such as chromium, which

will help to reduce the sweat. As for smell, most obnoxious body odours emanating from the underarm area can be simply countered by cleanliness, as the bacteria will start to smell when they come in contact with the oxygen and go rancid, which takes a bit of time. One of the best, and importantly fragrant neutral, deodorants is Triple Dry by Linden Voss (easily available in London at Boots) If your problem is odour and it seems to emanate from not only your underarms, you may need to correct your diet accordingly.

Diets high in garlic and onions should be avoided as these smells can come out throughout the body as it eliminates through the skin.

Those who feel their perspiration is often brought on by nervousness should include more vegetables in their diet as these foods feed the nervous system and calm the nerves. Drink more vegetable juices than fruit juices until the nerves settle and calm. Then slowly introduce fruit juices, avoiding citrus juices in the beginning. You may need a supplement to help give the nerves extra support such as a homeopathic Magnesium Phosphoricum.

HANDS   Check you finger nails daily to see that they are clean, tidy and short. What ever it takes for you to keep your nails clean, do it. Even if you have to carry a nail brush around with you. Clean hands and nails are always necessary and noticed, whether you see people looking or not (yes, professionally and socially)

MOUTH Bad breath is often caused by bad teeth or the state of your stomach. It is best to have your teeth checked regularly and ask your dentist or hygienist to help you with your brushing and flossing techniques. Flossing teeth should be done at a minimum of once a day to keep small gaps free of food debris and pungent plaque deposits.

The tongue should also be regularly brushed or scraped with a tongue cleaner when you brush your teeth (twice a day minimum, right?) and rinse thoroughly with an antibacterial mouthwash. If your breath is still bad it may just be something temporary like having an empty stomach. Try eating an apple for fresh breath or chew parsley if the meal was especially pungent (be sure to discreetly check your teeth before giving any broad smiles!)

MANNERS Good manners are essential for men to appear truly attractive and you can be sure your clients will love you just that bit more if you can be thoughtful and well mannered on a job. Don't make it appear as if you are trying too hard to be well mannered, as this may come off as being a bit slimy or false. Genuine charm is easily noticed and the best way to develop charm is to be intelligent enough to be thinking

on the job and try to remember their names and use them during the day. Write them discretely down in your diary if you can't remember them, it will help you to get the names right.

Hold elevators for people, open doors for women (including unattractive female work colleagues, not just the female models!!) and generally be thoughtful.

No one is asking you to make coffee for everyone in the studio but listen attentively to his or her stories and laugh in the appropriate places. Let the girls change in plenty of privacy, this will make them feel secure around you, don't leer or stare at their breasts when you are talking to them, look them in the face and eyes.

Don't tell raunchy or disgusting jokes, I know you may get a great laugh at the pub but girls and women clients don't want to think about you and relate you to the ugly pictures you created for them in their heads, leave the graphic jokes for social situations.

Try to be helpful, carry bags when you can, not only for the women but helping others who you see have more than a load, will be noticed or mentioned along the way and is overall expected, if you want to be considered as good mannered. It always leaves a good impression on clients, photographers, stylists and makeup artists alike. You NEVER know where your next job can come from so treat everyone on the job with respect whether you like them or not, they are all human beings and are there for a reason, so try to make it an all around happy experience and it will be a pleasure for everyone to have you around. This trait alone can help you score the next job and be recommended by those that work with you, to others. It is all money in the bank!

THE OTHER BITS Some things are specifically applicable to men only and yes, we ARE talking body hair. Just because you had a stubble at the casting, doesn't mean the client will want it on the day. Always get your specific instructions about shaved or unshaved before arriving at your job or meeting the team on location. You don't want everyone waiting around for you to shave or your rash to settle down. Some clients will specify if they want a 3 day growth or not or shaved chest and stomach hair or not, but other things should always be kept neat and trimmed. Leg, arm, chest and crotch hair should be evenly trimmed with an electric trimmer. These are very inexpensive and come with adjustable length attachments. It is up to you how short the hair should be, but it should look regular and natural and should not be prickly and irritating. Squirming around and having short curlies sticking through your underwear should, at all costs, be avoided.

After trimming your hair, jump into the shower to wash off all the loose hairs and remove any rough or discoloured skin on elbows, knees, heels and feet with a pumice stone. You may need to soak the area in the bath if it has never been tackled before or done recently, but don't be too vigorous on elbows if you are new to the pumice stone concept. Removing too much skin can leave elbows sore, use your judgement until you are used to it. Lather a good body moisturizer all over your body paying special attention to the elbows, knees and heels.

For shaving your face, use Noxema, Elemis or Nivea range. They are great for sensitive skins and wet shaving with a Nivea moisturizer lotion will help beat razor rash. (change razors regularly) Boots also have a good, cheap range. This may all sound time consuming but to get in form always takes a little time and effort. Upkeep is easy, and needs little attention when grooming is so crucial.

When on a job whether it is underwear or a nude picture try to keep the nudity down to a minimum. You may indeed have the body of a Greek God but excessive nudity is not well mannered and will not make you appear free spirited or open. In a work situation it is always better to err on the side of discretion.

KEEPING UP THE UPKEEP The initial effort may seem a bit time consuming but the upkeep for men is pretty simple. The trick is to keep things in the area of upkeep and not let them slip. This demands attention to detail and not obsessing to the point where you make it worse (case in point: eyebrows)

Your hair should be regularly trimmed by the same person if you can, so they know exactly which length is the best length for your clients. Always keep hair immaculately clean for jobs as you never know what look the client will want for the job and you may waste time by putting the wrong kind of product in your hair before a job. Leave it up to the hair stylist. Dandruff and dull hair should always be treated and taken care of before the job. Check the previous chapters on keeping your hair nails and skin in tip top condition.

AND LIPS Dry cracked lips are definitely not appealing and can look really dreadful in a picture. A makeup artist will be able to help you, but the results are not always the best when the skin is already dry and peeling off. Your lips should never get to that point. Gently brush your lips with a soft toothbrush, like a child's toothbrush, with warm water at night to remove the dead skin. Immediately follow with something healing and softening for lips before you go to bed, so it has plenty of time to soak in and do it's job. Use it when lips are wind burned and generally suffering from the cold weather or too much sun. (try dot balm available from website through feedback)

WHAT TO TAKE ON THE JOB   Grooming is often all that is required for men and if the client has a low budget, this may mean there is no makeup artist on the job. Always be prepared with your shaver or razor & foam, hairbrush, travel deodorant/antiperspirant, hair product and trimmer. Eye drops, like Optrex Red Eye, are essential due to travel and time zones.

Your makeup needs may just be a little concealer for a surprise pimple or under eye circles, your dot lip balm and powder. Powder is very important so find one that isn't too highly pigmented and looks cakey. Look for one that says "Transparent" You can get some product recommendations from some of the good makeup artists you work with. Use a large brush to apply powder.

PLUCKING EYEBROWS   Men's eyebrows need to look natural and unplucked. Keeping them trimmed regularly will make it easy to maintain the shape. For those of you who have never tackled your eyebrows before, there are a few general rules. The most important rule is; get up close to see what you are doing NOT to make the shape of your eyebrows. One or two hairs taken out at the wrong place can take ages to grow back in and can spoil the whole "look".

When taking out hairs between the brows, make sure you leave a natural edge to the two brows, so they look like they naturally ended there. If there is a sharp cut off point it will look obvious they have been plucked from even a long distance, this is really important! If your brows are really thick and bushy or have dark patches, just thin out the brows, or the dark patches by taking hairs out in amongst the bushy dark bits. Be careful not to create any holes, just take out the hairs that are crowding the others, leaving the ones forming the shape. The shape of the brow should be determined by the inside and outside corners of the eyes and the height of the brows. If you were to draw an imaginary line from the outside corner of your nose, straight up to the inside corner of your eye (use a pencil to show the line if you like) the continuation of

this line is where your eyebrows should softly end. Now draw the imaginary line from the corner of your nose to the OUTSIDE corner of your eye. The continuation of this line is where the eyebrows should naturally end. Let the natural arch of the eyebrow be your guide as to how high the brows should be.

As a rule, eyebrows should not be plucked from ABOVE the natural brow position as we are always trying to create height, so as to open up the eye. A mans eyebrow shape should be strong, but not overpowering the face. If the eyebrow hairs are long, curly or completely unruly, it is possible to trim the hairs by combing them upwards towards the hairline and cutting the hair at an angle so as to imitate the natural point at which a hair usually tapers off.

The trimming of eyebrow hairs should be done in small increments, so as not to cut off too much, leaving the hair too short, sticking out at an unnatural angle, or looking blunt and obviously cut.

BEFORE

WRONG

IDEAL

ONE OTHER BIT   Some male models that do a lot of underwear jobs sometimes use a thin rounded shoulder pad to put inside the front part of the underwear pants to create a smooth bulge. This may not always be necessary as most fabrics are not super thin and most clients are not too conservative. Check with the stylist on the job if you are unsure whether to use something or not. Always arrange yourself neatly and privately. If it is impossible to remove yourself from the set discreetly, turn away from your crew to make the necessary adjustments.

FINAL

„Luck is what happens when preparation meets opportunity." Seneca

There are some issues that do tend to cross male and female boundaries and as a professional, out in the work force, it is up to you to make the most out of your opportunities. Wasting the chances you have in life is a sign of immaturity, insecurity and frankly, stupidity. As it is with many things in life, there are obvious opportunities with which you will compete with all the other millions of people and then there are the NOT so obvious opportunites. As the first century Roman Seneca said "Luck is what happens when preparation meets opportunity". It is up to you to lay the ground work in your presentation, to make the most of your opportunities, seen or unseen. Clients have many projects that they work on, they know a lot of other people with whom they discuss talent as well as stylists, photographers and hair & makeup people. Your presentation, behaviour and professionalism will be a strong place for you to influence and use to impress.

Modelling is a highly competitive, small and constantly fluid niche in the fashion business. Certain "looks" can go in and out of fashion very quickly and it will be up to you to stay on the ball with your presentation and seize every opportunity to grow your client base and business.

Beside all the issues this book has already covered in the previous chapters, it is worth mentioning some of the fatal mistakes people who enter the modelling business constantly make.

SELF STYLING Clients do not necessarily have the skill to see through the "look" that you have created this morning to go to your castings. This is why they need a portfolio of your different looks to help them imagine you in a certain character, role or situation. Dress in a way that can create a blank canvas for the client to imagine you in their particular story. Too much jewellery, hair product or crazy clothes can distract a client from actually looking at YOU, and that is what you are trying to sell. What or who you are in your private life is completely up to you, but you are trying to be appealing to your client who has the decision to hire you or not. Help them to make the decision easier. Turn up the grooming but turn down the styling.

For guys, build up a basic wardrobe of plain black/white T-shirts, shirts and slim legged trousers/ denims and a well fitting suit. Even if you are quite young, a suit will instantly make you look sophisticated, intelligent and smooth. If your booker suggests you wear a suit it is

TIPS

usually for a very good reason, as they have an inside scoop on what the client wants and will find appealing. Not wearing a suit to a casting when the booker has specifically suggested it, will send a message to your agent that you are indifferent about getting paid work and frankly, if you don't care about it, then why should they?

BINGE DRINKING We all like to go out and have fun with our friends, but there is something you should understand about binge drinking and modelling. They DON'T mix. It may seem fairly obvious that drinking/smoking and eating junk food are not good for your looks, but the occasional indulgence will not turn you into Frankenstein overnight. What we are talking about here is binge drinking, more than 5 units of alcohol on one given occasion. Whether you have castings or a job the next day there is no way you will get away with it. Firstly, no amount of chewing gum, teeth brushing or showering is going to cover the smell. You can delude yourself all you like but clients will smell it, and will label you with "unreliable" and "unprofessional" faster than the door closes behind you. If you had a job with hundreds of thousands of Pounds / Euros riding on it, would YOU take the chance on someone you instinctively thought wasn't up to it? Not if you were a professional at your job. Alcohol weakens the liver and digestive systems. The liver is responsible for metabolizing fats in your diet but it turns alcohol into acetaldehyde. It effects the body by degenerating cell tissue, causing fatigue and poorly functioning organs as well as affecting blood sugar and stimulating adrenaline which in turn stimulates a powerful hormone called cortisol, which controls the adrenaline. In simple terms it makes you age at a rapid rate. Not just on the outside but on the inside as well. You are deliberately giving yourself a major head start to illness and old age, as alcohol actually loads the body with toxins, stresses it out and makes it ugly prematurely and you just hit yourself with a massive overdose of it. Good luck being a model.

HEALTH Blue hands, spotty skin and a short temper? We all know the stories about models smoking cigarettes and drinking coffee to stay slim but for those of you who are already in the business, you know from your own observation that the key to longevity and glowing good looks is dedication to keeping a balance in your life, That goes for food, fun, family and just about everything else in life. Dicipline also builds a strong character. As long as you eat and drink 80% healthy, the 20% can be what you like. Once you feel the difference in how good, whole foods make you feel, you will prefer them. Having a clear head, plenty of energy, a happy mood and less colds and flu is such a bonus for being a model. You get to enjoy your experience totally and infect others around you with your good mood and easy nature. This in turn makes you popular and as an incentive, the pay off is getting rich. Could it get any sweeter?

FAVORITE RECIPES

Variety is the **spice of life** and it is also **good** for your **health!** Mix it up ...

THE BOMB STIR FRY Soak a cupped handful of mung beans and the same amount of lentils in separate bowls overnight in pure, filtered, cold water. Drain them of the soaking water and rinse them when you are ready to cook. Bring to the boil a pot of salted water as you would for pasta. Firstly add the mung beans and cook for about 4or5 minutes, then add the lentils. Cook for a further few minutes or until the beans and lentils are firm but cooked through (al dente) While the beans are cooking you can wash and slice a leek. Fry the leek gently in a tablespoon of olive oil. Chop some broccoli (including the stalk) into small bite size pieces, add to the frying leek and mix around until the broccoli has a light coating of oil and has started to warm up (around 3 minutes) Add a small amount of water (2-3 tablespoons) and add some crumbled stock cube to the water and mix it around so it dissolves and is mixed in well to the vegetables. Anything that cooks fast like zuccini slices, or mushrooms can be added now. Add a lid for 2 minutes or if you put in too much water, leave the lid off while the zuccini softens. (leave a little crunch) when the water is nearly gone, stir in the mung beans and lentils and some freshly washed spinach. When the spinach has wilted, serve immediately

BROCCOLI OR MUSHROOM SOUP Slice a medium size onion and fry it gently in a saucepan with a little olive oil and a small knob of butter. Don't have the heat too high or the butter will burn. Stir it a few times until it starts to become transparent. Brush any dirt off a good 2 handfuls (that you can pick up with your hand) of mushrooms. Finely chop them and add to the onions. Peel and chop 2 medium potatoes and add to the onion/mushroom mix until they are warmed through. Add nearly 500ml of filtered water and 2 small or one large stock cube of either beef or chicken. You may like to add some fresh thyme to increase the flavour. (if you add a bunch of stalks, tie it with kitchen string so it is easy to haul out before you puree the soup) Bring it to the boil and then turn down immediately to a slow simmer and cook until the potatoes are soft. Puree in a blender or mash the potato with a potato masher. Take off the heat and add soy milk to taste (about a cup)

(replace mushrooms for broccoli for the broccoli soup)

SNACKS Toast a piece of sunflower seed bread or use Kalvi crackers (the green packet is garlic) top with your choice or all...avocado, sunflower seeds, sliced raw mushrooms, tomato & sprouts.

KILLER SALAD Put 2 or 3 tablespoons of olive oil in the bottom of your serving salad bowl, add either a squeeze of lemon juice or 1/2 cap of apple cider vinegar and mix into the oil with a fork. Add chopped tomato, spring onion, cucumber, sliced red bell pepper or whatever you like. Add your salad/lettuce leaves, washed and spun of excess water when you are ready to serve. Chop parsley finely and put on to of the lettuce with sprouts, a sliced boiled egg and some sunflower seeds/pine nuts. Toss and serve immediately.

FRIENDS OF DOT DOT DOT

There are quite a few people who have helped and inspired the book Dot Dot Dot. Without some of these people the book would never have made it into existence, and without others it would certainly not be in the form you see it now.

Photographer Jens Boldt is possibly one of the most talented photographers I have ever had the pleasure to work with. His coolness, humility and respect for models makes him a dream to collaborate with. Check out his web site for pictures to inspire you.
www.jens-boldt.com

Volker Wenzlawski shot the step by step nail pictures with Jennifer Hansen, the hand model. Having a professional hand model and a photographer such as Volker is such an honour and we had such a fun day shooting. Volker is also a really great talent and I felt so excited to have my two first choices as photographer and model both say yes to doing the shoot!
www.wenzlawski.com

Stacy Lobb from Model Management and Steven Priebe from Body &Soul are the two models in the Casting Your Line editorial. Stacy is one of the sweetest, smartest models I ever met. Being beautiful as well, hardly seems fair, but just to make it worse she is also really funny.
Steven Priebe is also an adorable guy but I wouldn't want to embarass him infront of his other Aussie mates, so I will just leave it at that!

Michael Dye was the stylist for the Casting Your Line editorial and is a formidable talent with a portfolio full of Vogue and famous faces. To have Michael style for our shoot shows the nature of Michael as a person. Generous, unpretentious and patient. He mixed it up and pulled it together in a way that was fresh and achievable.
Michael is represented by Wood Associates in London.
www.wood-associates.co.uk

Raimund Fritsche is surely one of Europes best kept secrets. Truely an undiscovered talent that has yet to find his true potential. Our beauty photographs for the chapters on Skin and Hair are not only beautiful, but we had a great time shooting them and to Raimund we are eternally grateful for the humour and talent that he shared with us.
We say, the sky is the limit and he'll get it.

Lightning Source UK Ltd.
Milton Keynes UK
29 December 2010

164963UK00006B/60/P